Crop Circles, Cows, and Crazy Aliens

Blue Moon Investigations

Book 8

Steve Higgs

Table of Contents

A Visitation. Tuesday, November 8th 2203hrs

In the darkness of the countryside, the creature crept forward. Through its visor, it could see the lights of the building ahead.

A light rain was falling. Drops hit the creature's protective suit but could not penetrate it. Underfoot the muddy soil squelched, the weight of the creature displacing the dirt as it walked.

It crept forward, the sound of its breathing loud in its ears inside the protective helmet. Nervously, it scanned about, hoping to make contact with the lifeforms that inhabited this place. It was not so bold as to dare to approach the dwelling it could see between the larger buildings. No, timidly it hoped it would be seen.

It had kept to the shadows as it approached, now though, to get any closer it would have to step into the light. It wanted to see inside the house. Light came from within, and noise too. Faint sounds of voices.

Crossing the expanse of moonlit yard, it could feel the unnatural surface of the concrete beneath its feet. It was nearing a window, planning to take a look inside when suddenly the door opened, pinning the creature in a shaft of light.

Frozen, it watched the new hole in the building. A human emerged. It was calling something, the voice high pitched, 'Here, Kitty. Puss, puss, puss.' A female of the species and clearly pregnant.

The woman was looking about but had not yet looked up. When finally, she did, her mouth was opening to call again. Like the creature, she froze, but it was momentary. As her eyes widened, she started to scream. The noise pierced the silence of the night, jolting the creature into motion. The protective suit it wore limited its range of motion, but it hurried away as fast as it could.

A second voice called after it, deeper than the first, but did not pursue. As it left the buildings behind, the creature inside the suit allowed itself a smile of elation. Seeing the inhabitants of the farm had been terrifying but exhilarating. It had been a necessary part of the plan – it needed to be seen, to be recognised for what it was.

It had no way of knowing what the inhabitants might now do, but it was confident it had set in motion a series of events that would enable it to achieve a glorious goal.

Waking up this morning, it felt like a big day. The 8th of November had been the last official day of my career in the Kent police service. That I had handed my uniform and ID card in more than a week ago, didn't change that this was the first day that I would not be paid for my service since I was twenty-one years old.

In the years that I had amassed in uniform, I had earned a pension. Not a big one, and it would be not until my fifty-fifth birthday that I saw any sign of it, but it was there tucked away, nevertheless.

I was scratching to find positives from the experience. It was a lot like attending ballet classes when I was four. I did it because I had seen it on TV and convinced myself that it would be glamorous and fun and then had tried really hard because I believed that success relied upon me giving it my all. In the end, I had given it up because I found it neither glamorous nor fun and the only reward I got was blisters. Being in the Police had been exactly the same.

It was behind me now though. My life had moved on. In some ways at least. I was still the same me; determined to be self-sufficient and capable while quivering inside half the time.

I caught myself in the act of self-doubt and berated myself out loud. 'Snap out of it, Amanda.' I sat up in bed and stared at the mirror.

My new job, working for Tempest Michaels at the Blue Moon Investigation Agency, was different every day. I was telling myself that this was a positive thing, even though I was not entirely certain it was. There was a part of me that wondered if maybe I should learn accountancy because it would be mundane and safe. Safe sounded good because in the few cases I had already pursued in my new job, I had been threatened, tasered, stripped naked and almost killed. Some of those on more than one occasion.

My adrenalin was getting employed more often than I had anticipated. My boss kept assuring me that this was not normal and that most of the cases he had investigated since opening the business had involved hours

3

of research and careful deduction, rather than chases, fights and stitching wounds closed.

That was not my experience thus far.

I swung my legs out of bed, then propelled myself up and into the cool air. My first task was to shut the window as my skin was already goose-pimpling from the November temperature coming through it. I found I had to have the window open at night – it was too warm otherwise, even with the heating off. Once up though and without the sanctuary of my duvet to maintain my warmth, it needed to close.

In the living room, I turned on the TV, powered up a news channel and flicked on the kettle for coffee. I had elected sleep over gym but forced myself to perform some basic stretches and exercises. Yoga poses, and some calisthenics would do for today.

At twenty past eight, with coffee, a pint of water and a blueberry bagel in my belly, I set off for work. I needed a new case so this morning would involve reviewing enquiries, calling a few clients and determining which case or cases held the most merit. Case selection was more complex than solving the case itself according to Tempest. As a firm that investigated the paranormal, most of the enquiries we got were from complete whackos.

Just yesterday, James, the office assistant, had read me an enquiry from a man that claimed to be in possession of a demonic banana. Tempest had taken the time to email the man back with instruction to throw it away.

There was all too much opportunity to rip people off. Tempest could have sold the man a story about the dangers of demonic fruit, taken some tap water labelled as holy water and charged the idiot five hundred pounds for an exorcism. Of course, if that had been something Tempest might have entertained, I would never have taken the job with him. He was all about integrity, charging an honest fee and making sure we felt decent about the service we provided.

The service itself was often about picking up where police investigations could not continue. Some crimes did defy explanation, but more regularly there was no crime occurring, there was just a mysterious event that the client wanted unravelled. We had one such case on the books now – crop circles.

The client had first emailed us a few weeks ago. It was a something or nothing enquiry where they had something mysterious happening but didn't really know what they wanted us to do about it. Now it seemed to have escalated with additional odd occurrences. Yesterday, in the filtered emails that James sent Tempest and me, was a further email from the same client in which he claimed the cows' milk at the dairy farm he owned had turned luminous. This now was more serious for him than the loss of some wheat because his income stream had been shut off.

Thinking about my next case options in the car as I drove to the office, this one came out as a forerunner. Thankfully, the journey from my apartment to the office each day only takes a few minutes because I know the backroads to get there and avoid almost all of the early morning traffic. The main arteries leading into and out of Maidstone, where I live, and the surrounding Medway towns, all clog terribly at peak times. If I had an office-based job, I would most likely buy myself a pedal bike and cycle to work rather than fight the endless traffic.

My job though was far from office-based. Instead, I spent more than half my time out doing investigative work. There was research to do, but it was mostly performed by James because he was not only good at it but of the three of us, he was permanently in the office, so that we always had someone there to receive enquiries in person. The new office, which we only moved into two days ago, sat very visibly on Rochester High Street. Its prominence generated drop-ins where people walking by would stick their head through the door and make their enquiry in person.

The percentage of genuine enquiries to crazy ones actually seemed to be higher when made in person although we only had two days' worth of data to go by thus far.

I pulled into my parking spot a few minutes after eight thirty. I was the first one to arrive this morning. More usually James beat me and often Tempest too. I liked that I was the keen one today.

Inside, I powered up the lights and the coffee machine and turned on my computer before I heard footsteps echoing along the passage that connects the carpark with the main office.

'Morning.' Called James as he swished in through the back door. It opened next to my office, so he was instantly outside my door.

'Hi, James.' I had to look up to check what James was wearing. He liked to cross-dress. He was gay and mostly gender-neutral, but in the short time that I had known him, he had been dressed as a girl more often than not. Only in the last few days had the balance swung to boys' clothes. Today he had on black skinny jeans, a white shirt, black tie and black leather jacket with a pair of four-inch red stiletto heels that really complimented the whole ensemble. His hair was getting long and voluminous. The style this morning was swept from a side parting on the left to create a low hanging flick over his right eye. It was stuck in place with product. He also wore more make-up than me, which when you consider that he was trying to look like a girl and wasn't, came as no great surprise.

'You're in early.' He observed. 'Want some coffee?'

'I set the machine already.' I called after him. My computer had finished its boot up which allowed me to get started. I was surprised at how excited I was to get stuck into a new case.

I had spent some time checking back through the emails we had from the same client. There were four in total, the first of which was sent when it was only Tempest at the firm just over six weeks ago. I looked down at my notes. The emails were from Kieron Fallon of Brompton Farm in Cliffe Woods. There was a website link that I clicked as I dialled his number and noted both his name and that of the farm in my book.

'Kieron Fallon.' The voice that answered had a caramel twang to it. The image in my head was that of a tall man with broad shoulders, wearing green wellies over dark blue jeans, faded from wear, and a body warmer undone at the front and spattered with dirt here and there. At his feet was a sheepdog despite it being a dairy farm. I wondered how close to reality that image would be.

'Hi, Mr. Fallon. This is Amanda Harper of the Blue Moon Investigation Agency. I have an email from you asking for our help.'

'Oh, God. You couldn't pick a better time to call. The police are here right now but they are not taking us seriously at all.' He was burbling, his words coming in a torrent.

I had to interrupt him before he told me anymore. 'Mr. Fallon, hold on a moment. Why are the police there?'

'Why are the…? We had an alien outside our house last night, isn't that why you are calling?' He sounded confused now.

'No. I don't know anything about that. I was calling because I have an email from you. Something about crop circles and glowing milk.'

'Sorry. Sorry, yes, of course. You couldn't possibly know about our visitation last night. Sorry, Amanda, was it?'

'Yes.'

'Amanda, I have a serious problem here. We are being targeted by aliens and no one will take us seriously. The police won't touch the case and we are going to go bust in a few weeks if I can't sell my produce. How soon can you come?' He genuinely sounded desperate.

'Okay, Mr. Fallon…'

'Kieron, please.'

'Kieron. I need to do some discovery first, learn more about the case before I commit. Do you have time to talk now?'

'Um.' He hesitated. I had to wonder why. He sounded desperate to meet me a few moments ago and now he was less sure. 'I have to attend to something, but I can call back in a little while.'

He didn't expand on what it was that he needed to attend to, but I offered no argument and let him go. I believed he would call back soon enough. In the interim, I busied myself setting up my desk. I had brought a box of bits from home to make the office seem more like my own. A photo of my Mum and Dad went on the desk. It was from a few years ago and she would most likely not approve now as Dad was gone and she had moved on. I had some personal stationery bits, such as a stapler in the shape of a red, high-heeled shoe and an eraser in the shape of a pair of lips that had been a gift from Patience at some point in the past. The desk drawers had things in them, files and bits of paper from Dr. Parrish, the previous tenant. I removed them to the cardboard box I had used to carry my stuff and placed it back in the utility cupboard where we had put everything else.

I drained my second cup of coffee and sat purposefully in the big comfy chair behind my new desk. I was ready.

Now what?

I moved the mouse to bring the screen to life and reread the email from Kieron. That ate up less than a minute.

I needed another case to work on, multiple cases even, so that I would always have something to do and always have someone to invoice. Right now, I was earning the firm not one penny and my last case had been for a girl that could barely afford even our cut-price rate.

Thankfully, the phone rang. It was Kieron calling back.

'Amanda Harper.' I answered.

'Amanda, hello again, it's Kieron. Sorry about that. The police were leaving, and I have all manner of alien fanatics at my gates trying to get in to see the evidence. You said you had some questions for me.'

'Thank you for calling back so promptly. What evidence?'

'Huh?'

'You said alien fanatics were trying to get in to see the evidence.' I reminded him of his own words.

'Oh, yes. There is a footprint. Well, several actually, but one that is really quite well preserved. The police showed enough interest to photograph it but that was all. They kept asking if the intruder had stolen anything or threatened anyone. My wife and I had to keep repeating that it was an alien creature, that it didn't attempt to do anything and ran away as soon as Lara, that's my wife, saw it.'

I thought for a second. 'Is the footprint still there?'

'Err, yes. Why?'

'I think it will be worth preserving as evidence. Did the police not take a cast of it?' I asked.

'A cast?' He was being good enough to answer my questions, but it was obvious that he didn't know why and was growing bored of them already. He wanted results, not more questions. I sighed at how sloppy and dismissive the police had been and wondered how I would have acted had it been me that was dispatched to visit their alien encounter scene.

I changed tactic. 'I hope to get stuck into this case straight away, so please tell me more about it. Your email mentions crop circles and something about the milk your herd is producing.' I had the phone on speaker, but not so loud it would disturb James or be heard by anyone that came in the front door. It left my hands free to take notes, so with a poised pencil, I listened.

'I need to go back to the beginning I think.' He paused, gathering his thoughts, no doubt. 'About two months ago, just before harvest, we started finding crop circles in our wheat fields. They were just like ones I had seen on TV, large concentric patterns. When Richard, that's Richard Tanner, one of the other farmers in the co-operative, first found his corn laying down, he called Glen and me to come and have a look. Glen is the third farmer in the group.'

'Richard didn't know what to make of it and neither did I at first, but Glen's wife, she was walking around the field looking at the corn. She said, "It's all in a pattern." And we realised it was a crop circle. The odd thing was, all the corn was cut.'

'How so?'

'I looked it up, when crop circles are formed, the corn just ends up laying down in a pattern. Our corn was cut up as if it had been through a lawnmower.'

'Can you tell me what the date was?' I asked. It might be important later.

'Err, ooh, no. I can work that out though. Is it important?'

'I don't know yet, Kieron. Please continue.'

I heard him make a few hmming noises, 'So anyway, there was a crop circle in Richard's field. September 17th.' He announced suddenly. 'It was September. I think it was a Tuesday. I'll ask Lara, she'll know.'

'We can come back to it later, Kieron.' I wanted to hear about the cows.

'Well, next thing we knew there was another circle in another of Richard's fields a few days later, then I had one in mine and then some college kids turned up. They had heard about it, they said. Called it a natural art phenomenon that they wanted to record and chronicle. Chronicle, that was the word they used. I had to look it up.'

I interrupted again. 'Do you have their names?'

'I do somewhere.' I could hear him rummaging. 'Lee and something. Young lads they were. I'm not one for labels, but I guess most would call them geeks. Very thin and pasty, like they don't get outside very often. I've got their number somewhere. They asked me to call them whenever a crop circle occurred.'

I could get it later.

'Found it.' He said. 'Do you want it now?' I had him read the number to me. I still hadn't worked out what it was that he wanted me to investigate. I brought him back to the present. 'Kieron, did you lose a lot of your wheat from the crop circles?'

'What? Oh, no, not much. No, that's not the problem at all. The problem came when the cows started producing luminous milk. Strangest thing I ever saw.'

'When did that first occur?'

'Three weeks ago. It was just my herd to start with, then two days later it was Glen's, then a day after that it was Richard that called to say it was his as well. We called the feed supplier and grilled them about it, they changed the feed but that made no difference, we took the machinery apart and cleaned it all more thoroughly than usual. We switched them to their winter hay early. None of it made any difference.'

I had a question. 'Have you had the milk tested?'

'Yes. We sell the milk to a major supermarket brand, I called them, and they sent a chap to inspect it. Then he called a chap to take some samples. All they did though was assure us that it wasn't fit for sale and said we should call them when it is. I had the vet come out to inspect the cows.'

I was getting lots of detail. There was something going on at the farm and I would need to visit rather than write endless notes now.

I interrupted him again. 'Kieron, sorry for interrupting, I think it best if we continue this in person.'

'I haven't told you about the spaceships and the alien yet.'

Spaceships.

I bit. 'What spaceships?'

'If the crop circles and the milk wasn't bad enough, Lara ran into an alien right outside our house last night. That's why the police were here and there are lights in the sky most nights. I called the police, but they have been out half a dozen times now and are getting bored with me calling them. There's no crime, you see. Nothing has been stolen, no one had been hurt or threatened.'

'Did you see the alien, Kieron?'

He sighed. He had answered this question before. 'No. No, I saw something. It has become quite a point of friction. Lara swears blind that it was a creature in a space suit of some kind and got quite upset when I didn't corroborate her story. All I saw was a flash of something in the moonlight before it disappeared in the dark. I went after it, but there was nothing to see by then and I didn't have a flashlight with me.'

'What do you think it was, Kieron?'

He was silent for a second. 'I don't know what to think. There is a lot of strange things happening here. I tell you what I know though. If we don't start selling milk in the next few weeks, I am going to go bust. Me and Richard I reckon. I am eating through bank loans and savings and the bank already said no to any further loans. Glen has money of his own. Savings or something so he might be alright for a bit longer, but I need this mystery solved.'

I guess that was I where I came in.

'Mr. Fallon, can you give me an hour? I need to do some research, but I will call back before lunch and arrange to visit if I am going to take the case. Either way, I will call back.' I was desperate to take the case but didn't want to appear so.

'Okay.' He said, disappointment heavy in his voice.

We disconnected. I had two pages of notes. I needed to see what had been reported in the papers and learn whatever I could about crop circles, cow tampering and alien invasions quickly. It felt like a real case, one where I could make a difference to the client when (if) I solved it.

I had butterflies.

I needed to start somewhere, so I called the mobile number for Lee, one of the college students Kieron had described and thought about what I wanted to ask him.

He answered before I could coalesce my thoughts. 'Speak.' Was all he said. Was that any way to answer a phone?

He probably thought he sounded cool or was doing it to impress someone he was with. Nevertheless, I spoke. 'Good morning. My name is Amanda Harper. I am a private detective hired to investigate some strange events in Cliffe Woods. I believe you have...' The line went dead.

It sounded very much like he had hung up on me. I tried his line again, but it wasn't answered. It kept coming up as line busy, so I was sure he was rejecting the call. I sent him a text instead, in which I explained that he was in no trouble and I merely had an interest in *his* interest in the crop circles.

He would get the text, but I couldn't force him to read it or reply. I might need to track him down at the college if he was still there.

Pondering what to do next, I went to get fresh coffee and catch up with James. I was going to have research for him to do.

Then Tempest came through the back door, his dogs preceding him and with one of his friends in tow. I couldn't remember the friend's name though. It was another nickname, lots of his friends seemed to have them as if their own names were boring: Big Ben, Basic and whatever this chap's name was.

The next half hour was lost in conversation and explaining about the crop circle case I was almost certainly going to take.

Aliens in Kent. Wednesday, November 9th 1030hrs

I cracked my knuckles meaningfully as I sat in front of my computer. A swift google search supplied more information than I could sift in a lifetime. I had searched for crop circle theories. Seeing the amount of information available, I decided to circle back to it – see what I did there?

Smiling to myself, I tried a different search. Looking for alien sightings in Kent, I discovered that there wasn't much to discover. There had been a green mist seen over Tonbridge a few years ago and a large triangle had been reported over the sky not far from Ashford a few years before that. All the reports were sketchy and made by one person with the exception of the Tonbridge green mist which had been seen by thousands and even came with photographs. I read some of the articles because they were interesting, but there didn't appear to be anything I could learn from them that would be pertinent to the case.

I looked at the clock on the computer to see that ninety minutes had slipped away while I was reading. I called out to James in the main office, mostly to see if he was there because I couldn't hear him. When he answered, I got up and went to find him rather than summon him to me. It wasn't that kind of office.

'Can you do some research for me?' I asked.

He flexed his skinny arms in a comic show of muscle, 'It's what I do best.' He claimed. 'What do you need me to find?'

'Anything you can on crop circles and leading theories on what causes them, anything to do with alien sightings in Kent. More recent reports will be more pertinent and see if you can find any reports of cow's milk being tampered with.'

'Tampered with by aliens?'

I thought about that. 'I guess tampered with by anyone. I am not buying into the alien visitation theory, but I believe that someone is messing with the milk. Between cow fiddling, alien spacecraft sighting and crop circles, there is something very odd going on over at Cliffe Woods.'

James just nodded his agreement.

'I am heading out to see the client. There is a case to solve here so I will get the paperwork signed and start billing them.'

'Got everything you need?' He asked. He didn't expand on the question but was referring to cameras, recording devices and other gear that I might wish to utilise.

A quick mental checklist didn't reveal a discrepancy. At this early stage of my investigation, I doubted I would need anything. I was just going to meet the client and get an initial payment. I said I would see him later as I headed to the back door of the office, snagging my handbag from my desk as I went.

As I slid into my car, my phone rang. I pulled the door shut against the cold as I answered it and switched the car on to warm up. 'Amanda Harper, Good morning.'

'Amanda, this is Kieron Fallon.' Kieron sounded different than he had in the earlier calls. Where he had been frustrated and perhaps a little scared before, now he sounded upset to the point of tearful.

'Kieron I was just setting off to come to you. Is everything okay?'

He didn't speak for a few seconds and I was about to prompt him when he finally started talking. 'It's our neighbour, Tamara. She was killed last night.'

'Oh God.' I hadn't meant to speak. My response was automatic.

'The alien got her. The police left here suddenly about an hour ago. They just got in their car and sped off. I just got the call from the farm manager to let me know Tamara's body was found not far from the farmhouse there. It was her husband that found her.'

She was killed by the alien. I hadn't heard incorrectly, that was what my client had said. Regardless of what had happened, the police would still be there. I had to ask the question though.

'Kieron why do you think it was an alien that killed your neighbour?'

'Because she was frozen. It killed her with a freeze ray.'

I let the words sink in. We were used to dealing with weird, it was our wheelhouse you might say. However, this was threatening to be a level beyond. My foot twitched with indecision but I needed a case and the firm needed to raise invoices so I had to get going.

'Mr. Fallon, I am heading to the scene now. Can you give me the address please?'

There had been storms about this week and it was still drizzling lightly on the drive to Cliffe Woods. I was familiar with the route to get there but could not recall having ever been to the village itself before. As my wipers did their best to swish the rain away, I followed the signs through Strood and out into the countryside. It wasn't far to go but it also wasn't a straight line, the road followed the contours around lakes and rivers and narrowed to a single-track lane many times. Twice I had to stop and back up to a passing point when I came face to face with a tractor.

The danger of more farm vehicles slowed my pace.

About halfway there, my phone rang. Caller ID on the screen in my car told me it was Patience calling. 'Hello, Patience.' I answered as the call connected.

'What up, skinny biatch?' she replied. Patience Woods is a former police colleague that is still serving as a uniformed officer. She is black, she is loud, and she is taking a week off following a brief bout of kidnapping last week.

Her choice of salutations was generally different from mine. Different to everyone's for that matter but despite the colloquialisms, I knew what the question meant. 'I am fine, thank you, Patience. I am investigating a case in Cliffe Woods.'

'Cliffe Woods? There's nothing there. It's all farmland. What kind of case have you got in Cliffe Woods?'

'Aliens.' I replied, unsure how she would react. Patience, unlike me, was ready to believe in everything.

She surprised me with her response though. 'Aliens,' she scoffed. 'There's no such thing. Even I know that.

'So, how are you feeling? What are you doing with your time off?' I asked, changing the subject.

'I'm bored,' she announced. 'Everyone else is at work, I can't afford to go away anywhere and there is only so much daytime TV I can watch.' I wondered if she was going to volunteer her services to assist me and worried about whether her help was a good thing. Instead of offering to work with me though she said, 'I need a man.' She paused, then corrected herself. 'We need men. We need someone nice to take us out and make us feel like ladies.'

'Not planning to see Big Ben again?' I asked. She had enjoyed a very brief fling with a friend I had met through Tempest. He was a decent enough guy, but he went through women like there was no tomorrow. It made him a perfect match for Patience.

I could hear her think about her answer. I was nearing my destination and had to pull in once more to let a tractor through. By my window, a cow put its head over the hedge and stared at me. I locked eyes with it as it chewed. I liked cows. They had nice eyes. Brett had nice eyes. My recent failed attempt at a relationship with Brett Barker was behind me, but his face kept drifting uninvited into my thoughts.

'I don't think Big Ben falls into the category of men one gets to date.' She admitted reluctantly, breaking my train of thought. I thought it more likely that he had simply refused to entertain the idea. 'Anyway, that's not what I called for, white chick. I wanted to make sure you were set for Saturday night.'

'Saturday night?' I echoed. Saturday night? What was I supposed to be doing on Saturday night?

'Girl's night out?' Patience prompted, exasperation dripping from her tone.

Oh yeah. I had forgotten all about it. I decided to lie. 'Yes, of course, I am completely ready. I have my outfit picked out and everything.'

Patience didn't believe me. 'Mm hmm. What're you wearing then?' She called my bluff.

'Err, jeans and a satin halter neck top.'

'The satin top from Hobbs? The blue one?'

She had bought the lie. 'Yes, that one.'

'Not a chance, babe. We are going out to meet men. I don't want you cramping my style in your going-to-the-library outfit. I want you in something that has spaghetti straps and a skirt that stops above your knees. I'm broke, so I need you to look slutty and available so that boys buy us drinks.'

I sighed. 'I'm not sure I have anything like that in my wardrobe.' That was probably a lie too. In truth, I quite fancied going out for a fun girls' night. Some dancing and a few drinks sounded good, but I wasn't interested in having men pester me for my number all night and I knew Patience would literally pimp me out for a rum and coke.

'I'm certain you can find something, sweetie,' she replied. 'Eight o'clock at Bar Nineteen. Okay?'

I conceded. I would wear the jeans and satin top anyway. It would be too late for Patience to do anything about it by the time I got there.

She bid me a good day and disconnected.

I had arrived at a tee junction and was no longer sure which way I wanted to go. I had the postcode for the farm but out here in the countryside, postcodes were a lot less reliable than they were in the towns. I didn't want to take a wrong path and have to perform a three-point turn in a tight space or have to reverse back half a mile because it was too tight to turn around.

Looking left and right, neither direction looked promising. The village of Cliffe Woods was behind me, I had gone through it while talking to Patience. Calling it a village though was a stretch. It might be better described as a hamlet. It was barely more than a collection of houses and a pub. I was unlikely to find anyone there to give me directions, so I flipped a mental coin, chose right and turned left because I was bound to have guessed wrong.

The theory of always getting a fifty-fifty guess wrong held true as turning left was the right way. A wooden sign announcing Larson Farm hove into view and barely thirty seconds later a turning led me to the farm itself. Behind me, in the field opposite the entrance to the farm were several tents. It didn't look to be a camping site though and there was nothing here that could possibly attract people unless their hobby was to get as far from civilisation as possible and sit in a damp field.

Were the people there more of the alien fanatics Kieron had described?

The road leading up to the farm was muddy. There were large chunks of dirt in the shape of tractor tyre treads flung all over it and the whole surface bore a slick coating of wet, brown gunk. The smell didn't hit me until I opened my car door though.

I imagined that country folk would laugh at city people being bothered by the natural scent of the countryside, but I swear if it had been any stronger, I could have cut it into chunks. It took my breath away and made me gag.

I slammed the car door shut again and shoved my face next to the car freshener thing hanging from my rear-view mirror.

Ahead of me was a small gathering of people in rain macs and anoraks. They were outside the fence that bordered the farm and I would have guessed that they were the alien spotters even without one holding a sign bearing the legend, "come to earth, we're friendly".

The noise from my car door shutting caused the crowd to turn around and look in my direction. I was not considered interesting though, their attention drifting back to the farm almost immediately.

I got out of my car after preparing myself for the olfactory onslaught and walked up to the gate. It was closed to keep the crazies out. In the distance beyond the buildings, I could see the familiar white tent of the forensics team. The coroner's van along with three police cars was parked at the edge of the farmyard ahead of me. If they were still here, then the body had not yet been moved. I crossed my fingers and said a silent prayer that CI Quinn wasn't on the scene and someone I knew would be.

The nearest farm building was little more than thirty feet away, where I could see two men working. I called out to get their attention.

The man shook his head no, telling me in short that I was to stay out. I opened the gate and let myself in anyway. I would get nothing done by being timid. He stopped what he was doing with visible frustration, stood up and started making his way towards me.

'I'm Amanda Harper.' I said before he closed the distance to me. 'I have been hired by the three owners to investigate the strange events here.' I handed him my card.

Without speaking, he stared down at the card, reading it. It was shiny and embossed and had my name written on it with the words **Paranormal Investigator** in bold type beneath. He had been wearing gloves to do whatever it was he had been doing so his hands were clean. He didn't offer one to shake though. Instead, he came to a decision, inclined his head in the direction of the police cars and the tent and started walking. I was expected to follow.

'I'll take it from here, thank you for your help.' The man went back to his task. Ahead of me, the uniforms were milling around. I took a straight line toward them, hoping to make out a familiar face before I got there.

'Amanda.' Called out Brad Hardacre about a second before I called his name. We had spent hours in squad cars together over the years. He was one of the good guys, although he was a bit of a joker and didn't take himself seriously enough to ever make a decent career from the job. He had a big cheesy grin on his face. 'Amanda, are you here to catch an alien?'

The uniforms around him had heard him speak and turned around to see who he was addressing. There were five in view including a Sergeant that I didn't recognise, but the other four were familiar. Kent police were thousands strong but mostly regional, so you saw the same faces plenty of times.

22

'Hey, Brad. Hi, everyone.' I approached as if I was supposed to be there, offering Brad my hand to shake but he wrapped me into a hug instead.

'I heard about the voodoo thing. Hey, guys.' He said as he turned to his colleagues, one arm still around my shoulders to present me. 'This is Amanda Harper, the one that caught the Magdalene King.'

'Yes, Brad.' Replied a brunette woman. My memory was telling me her name might be Megan. 'She was all over the TV making that dick Quinn look stupid.'

'That's enough of that, Jones.' Admonished her sergeant. He turned his attention to me. 'How can we help you, Miss Harper?'

'She's here to catch the alien.' Brad said while making spooky noises with his mouth.

I offered my hand for the unnamed sergeant to shake. He looked at it, before somewhat reluctantly bringing his own hand up to meet mine.

'I have been hired by the farmers to look into the events here.'

'You don't think we can manage? You believe you are better suited to investigate this woman's death?' He was being confrontational.

'The death is a new development. They hired me to find out why their milk glows. There have been odd occurrences here for months now and the police have visited many times already. I only took the uniform off recently, so I know why it is not possible to commit resources to look into milk tampering.'

This placated him somewhat, his demeanour softening. 'You are saying you are here by chance, not because a woman has been killed?'

'Not exactly. I was coming anyway. My client believes he had been visited by aliens, that they have created crop circles near here and are tampering with his milk. When he called me an hour ago it was to tell me that there had been a death at the hands of the aliens. Was the victim frozen?'

23

'Yes, she was.' Answered Brad, drawing a hostile glare from his sergeant.

'I'm not here to interfere. There is something happening here though which is outside of your remit and which I have been employed to investigate. Something dubious is occurring at the farms in this cooperative and it seems likely to me that it is all linked with death. I know the victim was frozen.' I winced as he glared at Brad again. 'But assume I can rule out the possibility of a freeze ray toting alien as the murderer.'

'No one said murder and nothing is being ruled out.' He snapped back instantly. It was a standard policeman's answer to deny and confuse. I could follow up by asking if this meant he considered the alien freeze ray a possibility but I didn't. I wanted his help.

'Will you allow me to see the body?'

He opened his mouth to say no but at that moment the coroner stepped out of the tent. He was a man I had bonded with a couple of years back at a policeman's ball when we ended up at the same table and both stood up by our dates.

'Neville.' I called, which stopped the sergeant from speaking as he turned to see who I was now looking at.

The coroner had been looking at his phone, about to make a call perhaps but looked up, caught sight of me and broke into a broad grin.

'Amanda Harper. I heard you quit.'

I dismissed the sergeant by walking straight by him to shake hands with the coroner. Neville Hinkley was nearing retirement but was a handsome man that looked after himself and looked far younger than his advancing years might suggest he should. He had on white wellington boots and a forensic suit but was peeling his way out of it as he came towards me. The latex gloves came off with a puff of powder, a trace of which lingered on my hand after he shook it.

'I did quit. I'm here as a private investigator.'

'For this case? Want to see the body?' He asked.

'That's not appropriate.' Pointed out the sergeant, further eroding his authority as Neville didn't even bother to look his way.

I crouched down to peer inside the tent. I wasn't going in as I might contaminate the scene, but I could see enough to know that this was an unusual death. Some bodies curl into odd shapes in rigor but this one appeared to have been posed. Her feet were together, and her arms were out in front with her palms out and her fingers splayed as if she were pushing against something.

'Is she frozen?' I asked, wanting to clarify that point.

'Starting to defrost, but yes she has been frozen.'

'Do you think she was shoved inside a freezer?'

'Impossible to say but that would be my first guess. The officers scoured the premises looking for a freezer she might fit in but didn't find anything. If she was frozen, it was done off-site.'

I nodded. My case had changed drastically in the space of a few hours. What would this mean? Was I still investigating glowing milk? Was the death connected? I was happy to rule out an alien invasion but I felt certain the death, the milk, the alien and the crop circles would all prove to be linked somehow.

I stood up again. 'Thank you, Neville. I need to speak to the husband.'

'Anytime, Amanda. Just call if you need my help.' Neville had followed me back to where Brad and the others were milling about still. The sergeant had wandered off, I spotted him sitting in his car using the radio.

Pulling out my notepad, I sidled up to Brad. 'Brad has anyone interviewed the husband yet?'

'Of course. I think the two detectives are still in with him now.'

'Anyone I know?'

'It's Ben Hamilton and Maurice Beorby from Chatham. They've been in there a while actually.' He said, turning to look at the door of the farmhouse.

It opened as we were looking at it. A hand appeared around the door frame but then nothing else for a few seconds until a man in a cheap suit, followed by another dressed like the first's twin. They were the two detectives. I had seen them before but didn't know them and doubted they would recognise me. They were talking to an unseen person inside the house.

'Catch you later.' I called over my shoulder as I left Brad where he was and went to meet Glen Adongo, the owner of the farm and recently bereaved husband of the deceased.

The two detectives had left the farmhouse and were walking toward me. Mr. Adongo was closing his door.

'Mr. Adongo.' I called as I brushed by the men in their cheap suits. The closing door stopped and my client's head reappeared to see who had called him. 'Mr. Adongo, I'm Amanda Harper. I was hired by Kieron Fallon to investigate the strange events here and the impact it is having on your business. May I start by saying how sorry I am for your loss.'

'You had better come in.' He replied, resignation heavy in his voice. I had not intended to take up any of his time right now. I wanted to talk to him, but this felt like the wrong moment. He had invited me in though...

Glen was short at around five feet four inches tall and was what people would call lean. He looked like a long-distance runner but had a receding hairline that made his head look like a bullet. He was somewhere in his early forties and my best guess was that he was either Kenyan or Nigerian. My police training had included learning to spot different races from characteristics particular to them and to recognise different accents. I wasn't very good at it but I was certain he was of African descent. His movements were a little effeminate and it seemed out of keeping with the burly farmer image I had in my head.

He said, 'You'll have to excuse the mess. Today has not been the most organised.' As he led me through the house. I couldn't see any mess, but I kept my mouth shut anyway.

'So, you are here to find out why our cows are producing luminous milk, are you?' He asked as he flopped into an armchair set at a table. I was left standing and feeling awkward until Glen spoke again. 'I'm so sorry. Forgive my manners. Please have a seat.'

He jumped up to pull my seat out for me, but I waved him away as I set my bag down and slid into one of the ornate wooden chairs. As I opened my notebook I asked, 'What do you think happened to your wife?'

He closed his eyes and opened them again. 'The two detectives wanted to know the same thing. I can shed no light on what happened to Tamara. We went to bed together last night. When I woke up this morning she was missing. I didn't think too much of it at the time. She sometimes gets up to watch the sunrise, this is all still quite new to us as we only moved here in February. Usually though, if she did leave the house, she would return before breakfast. When I heard the first scream, I knew in my heart that it was her. That she was dead somehow and they had found her body.' I kept quiet while he talked as it is a golden rule to never interrupt a witness or suspect while they are telling you everything. 'I can't explain it. I just knew. So, when I went outside, there she was, frozen stiff and laying on the mud and grass where she had toppled.'

A single tear rolled down his left cheek, but he made no attempt to wipe it away. He looked sad or lost maybe. I had seen people look like him many times when delivering notice of death as a police officer. It was the least pleasant thing I had ever had to do and the task always left me feeling empty for hours afterward. I could only imagine what the bereaved felt at their sudden loss.

I had more questions that I wasn't going to seek answers for right now. I excused myself, thanked him for his time, repeated my sorrow for his loss and headed back to my car.

Outside, the sun was high in the sky but hidden behind a shield of thin grey cloud. To my right, the coroner's van was gone and a large white van from the forensics department was parked in the space it had vacated. Only one police car remained, the two officers with it electing to stay inside where it was warm. Their only purpose would be to keep people away from the body and the work the forensics chaps would be doing, so they were most likely right to hang out in their car.

I looked about. In front of me, opposite the farmhouse itself was a large shed that was open on two sides. I believed it to be the milking shed because I could see machinery inside that looked right for the job. I didn't know what I was looking at, but they had to get milked somewhere, right? It was devoid of life. Not a cow or a person within its confines.

To my left, was another building that could be anything. I was telling myself it might be important to learn more about the farms, how they are set up, how they operate, but I needed a guide to achieve that and not only was there no one around, but all the staff here had suffered a shock today. My questions could wait.

The impact of Tamara's death was probably felt less keenly at the other farms. I set off to my car.

'I have an appointment with Mr. Fallon.' I called. 'I'm here about the milk.' I had arrived at Brompton Farm, the home of Kieron Fallon but could not get beyond the gate, as just like Glen Adongo's farm, there was a small crowd of nutters gathered outside. Fortunately, there were a couple of farm hands within earshot just like there had been at Larson Farm.

When I called out to them, one spoke to the other, who then trotted off towards a steel-sided barn. The first came to let me through the gate, eyeing the alien spotters suspiciously in case any of them tried to get inside.

I got back into my car and drove through the gate to park near other cars as the man indicated. To my left, his colleague emerged from the building he had entered now accompanied by another man. This one was older and looked in charge. He was tall with broad shoulders. His outfit of dark blue jeans and body warmer over a check shirt was spattered with mud in places. On his feet, he had green wellies that had seen better days and a sheepdog trailed along at his feet, full of nervous energy as sheepdogs always are.

I was willing to bet my wages the man I was looking at was Kieron Fallon. He was exactly as I imagined him.

Just then my phone rang. I moved my hand to reject the call but saw that it was my mother. Kieron was approaching. I stabbed the button to quickly answer the call. 'Hi, mum.'

'Hello, Mandy. Have you got time to talk?' Mum often started conversations like that, have I got time to talk, but she never waited for an answer, so, true to form, she was already telling me about where she was and what her day ahead looked like.

I had to interrupt her. It took a few attempts.

'Mandy, what is it, dear? I was just telling you about Miami.' The disappointment at not being able to tell me her news was evident.

'I have to go, mum.' I told her for the sixth or seventh time. 'I have a client.' I explained.

'A client?'

'Yes, mum. A client. He is standing outside my car now. I have to go. I will call you back later.'

'But you're a police officer. You don't have clients.' There was a pause. 'Oh. God! Oh no. You're a prostitute now, aren't you?'

'WHAT?'

'I knew that silly police job wouldn't pay the bills.' She was muttering now and not listening to me at all. In the background, I could hear her shouting for her boyfriend.

'Mother.' I called down the phone through gritted teeth. 'Mother.' Still no answer. 'MOTHER!'

Finally, she came back onto the phone, still shouting something about me to John. 'Darling, I'll be on the next flight home...'

I managed to cut her off, 'Mother I am not a bloody prostitute. I am a private investigator. My client is a person with a case I am going to solve. For goodness sake.' She opened her mouth to speak again. 'I have to go, mum. I will call you this evening.'

I disconnected the call and savagely stabbed the button that would silence the phone in case it should ring again.

Kieron Fallon was waiting patiently next to my car, trying not to watch me while also keeping an eye on what I was doing.

Now that I was finished with my call, he tapped politely on the window. I opened the door and got out. 'Sorry, Miss, this is private property. Do you have business here?'

'Mr. Fallon, yes?' I offered him my hand.

'Oh, goodness, no. I'm the farm manager, Gordon. Mr. Fallon is a young chap. I'm afraid you won't get to see him without an appointment though.' The man's dog was leaning forward to sniff my leg. It looked as dirty as the owner. I moved away slightly.

'Mr. Fallon is expecting me. Please tell him Amanda Harper is here.'

Gordon looked slightly taken aback as if the idea that a woman might have business was preposterous. He was smiling at me like he was waiting for the punchline. Fortunately, the real Kieron Fallon emerged from the farmhouse. He was expecting a woman to visit and here I was.

Of course, I didn't know it was Kieron until he arrived and thrust out his hand. 'Hi, Amanda. Thank you for coming so quickly.' He turned to Gordon who was still standing where he had been, the dog next to his feet still looking up at me. 'I'll take it from here, Gordon. Thank you.' He said it in a positive way that sounded like he was praising Gordon for coming to see who I was, while also making it clear that the task was done, and he probably had other work to attend to.

Gordon was slow to respond though and clearly unhappy that he was being dismissed. 'I don't think you've got time to be socialising, Mr. Fallon.'

Kieron turned to face the older man, evidently less than happy with his attitude. 'Thank you, Gordon. I'll take it from here.' He repeated, this time with more force.

Gordon spun on his heel and strode away. The dirty dog lingered for a moment but soon realised his master was gone and went after him.

Kieron turned back to me. 'Sorry about Gordon. I got him with the farm when I bought it. I thought I was getting a real asset with his years of experience. Now I don't know how to get rid of him.'

'Is he a problem?' I asked.

'Sort of.' Kieron started walking back toward the farm buildings, indicating that I should walk with him. 'He has been here forever and knows that he knows everything. To start with, I thought I couldn't manage without him and made the mistake of saying it once. Now he argues with me about everything new I want to try. Drives me nuts.'

Kieron Fallon had a two-day stubble going beneath his almost black hair. His hair had been cut in the last week or less and complimented his tan skin. He sure was pretty. He had wide shoulders that tapered to a small waist, he was a shade over six feet tall and he had a smile that would light up a room. He had flashed it at me in greeting when he first walked over, and I almost had to grab the car to keep myself upright. He had the cutest dimples in his cheeks. Now he was walking away from me and I was looking at his muscular butt.

What is wrong with me?

I was behaving like a teenage girl, my hormones running unchecked. Had it really been that long since I got some? I did some mental maths and conceded that it had, in fact, been a while. It explained, to some extent, why I was drooling at the man-candy farmer.

At least that was what I was telling myself.

Kieron kept walking but turned his torso so he was looking back at me a few steps behind him. He slowed his pace so I could catch up but as he did so he pulled out his phone. 'I will let Richard and Glen know that you are here. I doubt Glen will visit, but it would be wrong to assume.' We had crossed the muddy apron of concrete that joined the farm buildings and were heading into a brick-built house that looked a hundred years old or more. The entrance door was low, Kieron had to duck as he went in. He had touched his phone and was speaking into it as I closed the door behind me.

He was talking to Glen, I had heard him say the name, but the conversation was brief. 'Can I offer you a drink? Tea perhaps?' He asked as he stuffed the phone into a back pocket.

'Yes, thank you.' Tea sounded good. It had been cooler out than I expected. It felt cooler here than it had in Rochester now that I thought about it. Was that normal? Was the countryside cooler than the city?

Kieron took a pace to the left and called through a doorway. A moment later, the yummy farmer's wife appeared. I hadn't noticed the ring on his finger, but it was obvious now that the heavily pregnant woman was waddling through the doorway and I remembered that he had mentioned his wife on the phone earlier.

'Lara this is Amanda Harper. She will be investigating the recent problems for us.' He said, his face still carrying the perfect smile that seemed to be permanent and his tone suggested that my arrival was the best thing ever.

'Right.' Mrs yummy farmer replied. 'You hired a cute, busty blonde to catch an alien that is poisoning our livelihood and probably plans to steal my baby. Of course, you did.' Clearly hiring me had not been her idea.

'If we don't solve this, love, there will be no farm.' He chided gently. 'Now be a love and make some tea, will you?'

She about-faced in the doorway and muttered something that sounded like it began with an F as she disappeared back through it.

Seemingly oblivious to his wife's mood, Kieron smiled brightly at me and indicated I should take a seat at the table and chairs arranged like a boardroom in what was a farmhouse dining-room setting.

'Glen and Richard will be along soon. I doubt they will mind if I get started though.' He powered up a laptop. 'I have some photographs to show you.' He said, swivelling the screen toward me. What I saw was pictures of crop circles taken from the viewpoint of someone standing inside them. Despite the close-up view, they could not be mistaken for something else. We talked about them until the tea arrived, Kieron's wife coming back through the same doorway with a mug in each hand just as two men and a lady came through the front door.

I recognised Glen and guessed correctly that the couple with him was Richard and his wife. She was introduced as Michelle and like Kieron's wife, she was pregnant, though not so far along.

'I suppose more tea is required.' Lara snipped as she went back out the kitchen door again. I wanted to feel sorry for her, but she was being a bit of a B**** in my opinion. I bleeped it out in my head because I didn't want to think about how tough it might be to be pregnant.

Richard's wife rushed after her, leaving the men to talk with me. I wasn't sure what this said about the emancipation of the housewife, but it was probably not a good thing.

The men all shook hands like old friends and then first Glen and then Richard shook hands with me. Glen had recovered his composure and tried to apologise for being upset earlier. I think he realised that it was unnecessary as he was saying the words and he trailed off, apologised again and took a seat at the table.

I took a seat as well and handed out a business card to each man. Like Kieron, Richard was in his early thirties and attractive in a burly way. I wondered if the baby his wife carried would be their first.

'I was just telling Amanda about the crop circles.' Kieron told his colleagues. 'It's the milk we need to talk about though.'

I interrupted him. 'If I may, I would like to learn some more about all of you and about your farms please.' I had flipped my notepad open once more and had my pen poised. The three chaps looked at each other, each of them waiting for someone to start speaking. 'Do you want to go first, Kieron?' I prompted.

'Sure. Richard and I went to university together in Cambridge where we studied agriculture and business. We bought the farms six years ago when first one, then the other came up for sale. At the time, the third farm, that's Larson Farm to the west, was owned and run by Sven Larson. Richard and I had a plan for a large cooperative of farms, but old Sven wasn't interested. We set up between ourselves and were able to secure a contract with one of the major supermarket chains for the supply of milk. We had borrowed up to our eyeballs, so it was a relief to finally be making a profit I can tell you.'

'Then Sven fell ill toward the end of last year and called us to say he was selling the farm and moving back to Sweden. We really wanted to buy it, the geography of it being so close to ours means that we can share manpower and equipment to achieve economy of scale with our overhead.'

Richard picked up the story, 'By making our business lean we were able to compete with other suppliers to win the contract. With another farm also producing, we could start making a healthy return. That was the original business model Kieron and I had worked out while still at Uni.'

'We couldn't afford the farm though.' Kieron said, taking over again. 'The banks just wouldn't lend us any more despite the strength of our predicted figures. It was heart-breaking.'

'So, we put out an advert.' Said Richard. Next thing we knew, Glen and Tamara called us and the rest, as they say, is history.'

'We bought the farm in January and moved here in February.' Said Glen, joining in for the first time. 'It was Tamara's dream to live in the countryside.'

'What did you do before this?' I asked him.

'I was a farmer in Kenya. Or rather, I grew up on a farm in Kenya, but it was confiscated under a government enforced land act when I was twenty-three. My father suffered a heart attack and died six weeks after the farm was taken from him. It had been in his family for six generations. I think he died of sadness. Mother had died two years before that, so I left

Kenya behind, disgusted that a ruler could do that to his people and came here. Like Kieron and Richard, I had to borrow a lot from the bank, but Tamara had money and she had a house in Knightsbridge which she sold. The money from that bought the farm and the loans covered the set-up costs to buy new equipment.'

Kieron started speaking again, 'With the milk no longer fit for sale, we will be owned by the banks in a matter of a few weeks unless we can find out what is causing it.'

I checked my notes, trying to be methodical. 'Tell me about your partners, please. Michelle and Lara. Where did you meet them, how long have you been married? That sort of thing.'

Kieron pointed to Richard so he would go first. 'We met them at a bar in Rochester. Kieron and I had just been into the bank to discuss more funds and been rejected again. This was in December when the farm was up for sale. We had met with Glen about a week before that, so we were getting excited about what the next year would hold. Anyway, the bank had turned us down, so we were drowning our sorrows instead. Ten minutes later these two girls walked in, came and sat next to us at the bar and we hit it off straight away.'

'Are you married?' It seemed like fast work if they were, but I had already seen the ring on Kieron's hand and could see one on Richard's now.

'I proposed when Lara fell pregnant. We set the date for May, but Michelle announced that she was pregnant in late April, so we changed it to a double wedding.' He talked about it with great happiness I noted. If he was this happy, what was with his wife?

'Tell me about the milk, please.'

'What about the alien your wife saw last night?' Asked Richard. 'She called Michelle.' Richard continued. 'I had already gone up to bed. But I heard the phone call and heard Michelle go out. I didn't think anything of it until she told me about it this morning. I figured she was checking on the livestock or something.'

Kieron started telling the tale from his aspect. Lara had gone to get the cat in, the first thing he knew about it was when she started screaming. He ran to the door in time to see the moonlight glint off something as it vanished into the dark field opposite the farmhouse. He couldn't tell what it was, but he called the police because his wife was borderline hysterical.

The police took their sweet time in his words. However, they showed up eventually. Two of them in a squad car, a man and a woman. They took a statement but didn't seem interested. When he found the footprint this morning, two different officers came. They seemed equally bored and detached, just going through the motions.

At that point, I interrupted to say, 'I need to see the footprint. I want to get a cast of it.'

Kieron turned to look out the window. 'It will get dark soon. It creeps up on us around here. We should go now.' He stood and pushed back his chair. 'Do you have a kit to make the cast?'

'In my car.'

As we walked toward the door, the wives emerged from the kitchen again. Lara held four mugs of tea, two in each hand. 'Where are you going?' She demanded to know. 'I just made tea. Because you bloody told me to.' She snapped.

'We won't be a minute, love.' Kieron said, his tone imploring her to stay calm. I slipped out the door as he went over to her. Making my way to my car I could hear a heated discussion coming from inside. Kieron was not doing well.

Directly across the yard from the farmhouse was the milking shed. It was very much the same design as the one at Glen's farm. To its left, was a field that now had crazy alien spotters hanging over its fence. Kieron caught up to Richard, Glen and me before we made it across the yard and led the way to the footprint.

'Sorry about that.' He said, referring to his wife's outburst. 'Late stages of pregnancy, everything's hard now.' No one said anything in reply.

The footprint was twice the size of mine and had been made by a boot, which is to say it was not the print of a bare foot. The boot though had three distinct toes, evenly spaced at the front and a fourth at the back. It was distinctly alien.

As I turned toward my car I said, 'I'll get my kit.' From the fence, the alien spotters were calling out to let them see it. I wondered how they had heard about it in the first place. It was something I would need to ask.

The kit was something Tempest had at the office. It was plaster of paris in a measured quantity with the bottle that contained the correct amount of water required to make the powder into the gloop I required. It came with a disposable plastic beaker. I had watched forensics guys use the police-issue equivalent at crime scenes in the past but had never touched one myself. This was a cheap version, but it would do the trick.

By the time I got back to the guys, I had the mix in the beaker and ready to pour. It would only be enough for a thin layer as the footprint was so big. I just hoped it wouldn't be so thin it broke when I took it out later.

While I poured the white mixture into the hole, I asked the chaps to begin telling me about the milk. Richard started by explaining how his farmhands had called him to his milking shed one morning. His milk was glowing. He had called Kieron and Glen over to his farm just so they could see it. It was so extraordinary. The milk was discarded. He was disappointed, but they thought nothing of it until it happened again the next day. Now it was a serious problem. They had called the older farm hands in and then they had called the local dairy cooperative administrator and then a representative from the farmer's union and none of them had any explanation, even an outlandish one, for the softly glowing milk.

The milk had been ditched again and equipment cleaned again and the next day it had happened yet again. The day after that it was Glen's milk as well and two days later all three of them were suffering.

Vets were called, the cattle inspected and given a clean bill of health. Their feed was discarded and replaced but nothing they did made any difference – the milk still came out of the cows with a luminescent green tinge.

'I think we have to sell.' Glen said when Richard finished speaking. He was almost begging the other two. 'If we quit now, we will still get a fair price. Hang on much longer and we will be in so much debt the banks will already own us.'

It was Kieron that responded first. 'I'm not moving, Glen. I'm not quitting. I have made a home here. Lara has a baby coming and this is where our little boy or girl will be raised.'

'Not if you go bankrupt first.' Glen snapped back.

Richard was trying to keep the peace. 'He has a point, Kieron. I know you don't want to sell. But we might have no choice soon. If we default on our loans, what then?'

We got onto talking finance, because, according to Richard, they *were* weeks from going bankrupt. We had walked back to the farmhouse and taken our seats again. The two pregnant wives drifted back to join us but mostly kept quiet, whether through disinterest or through the knowledge that their opinion was not wanted I couldn't tell. It had been cool out and I really quite fancied a hot cup of tea but I was damned if I was going to ask for one as the last round had gone cold before we returned.

While I listened and asked questions, I also noticed an odd dynamic at the table. The two wives had made a point of avoiding sitting near to Glen. Was it racism I was witnessing? Did they just want to not be near the bereaved man? Once I had noticed something was amiss, I couldn't help but see it. They wouldn't look at him, and when he asked a question or raised a point, neither one would engage with him. The husbands seemed unaware or oblivious. I kept my mouth shut and watched. Maybe it would be important later.

Maybe it was nothing.

The conversation reached a natural lull. It was Lara that filled the void. 'Tell her about the lights.'

I looked around the table at their faces. 'What lights?'

After two hours, the sun was dipping, and the farmers were anxious to get on with daily tasks they had been putting off. Richard had already made his excuses and left a few minutes ago when it became clear we were wrapping up. I had several pages of notes but no clue what to do with them. There were no obvious leads, but there were a few persons of interest I could talk to. At Kieron's begging, I was going to get straight on it. He was by far the keenest of the three to engage my services. It felt like the other two would have dismissed me if they could but didn't want to argue with Kieron. I believed them though when they claimed to be going bankrupt. Oddly, no one talked about the death of Glen's wife this morning as if they did not consider it to be connected.

I brought the subject up. 'Do you wish me to include your wife's death as part of my investigation, Mr. Adongo?'

He was startled by the question. 'I guess so.' He stammered as he looked at the others for support. Kieron placed a kindly hand on his arm.

'I will do some research tonight and will be back in the morning. I need to question your staff.'

'Why is that?' Glen asked.

'Because I need to rule out the very real possibility that this is an inside job. If someone is doing something to the cows, then they need to have access to them.'

'Didn't we just describe how it was aliens?' Lara asked, her voice incredulous.

'You did, but I'm afraid the likely explanation is something more terrestrial in nature.'

'Why do we need a paranormal investigator then?' She snapped back at me.

'Because no one else will take the case.' Kieron answered.

The final comment drew silence from everyone. I took that as my cue to leave.

As I left the table and Kieron walked me to the door, I could hear the wives muttering about being ripped off. They were not muttering quietly. Kieron's wife even accused him of falling for the pretty blonde's skinny arse.

I was glad to leave.

Outside it was already dark. The alien spotters were no longer visible by the fence, though I suspected they had only retreated as far as the tents I had spotted in the field across the road. It was only tea time, but evening was fast approaching, and it felt like time to go home and to see what James had found out this afternoon. Across the yard, I used my phone to light the way back to the footprint. The plaster had hardened already which allowed me to gingerly extract it from the mud without it breaking. In my bag, I had some evidence bags. They were basically zip-lock bags, but they proved handy when I found something that might have a fingerprint, or in this case, was covered in mud and cow poop.

As I made my way to my car, a light caught my attention. It had flashed on and then immediately off again like someone flicking a torch button quickly.

It came from over by the milking shed. I stopped to stare where I had seen the light. There it was again and now I saw a person move in the dark shadows. Were they trying to get my attention?

I took a pace towards the milking shed but was stopped by the sudden appearance of a man that had a cameraman right behind him.

'Hi. Jack Hammer, Alien Quest. Can I ask you a few questions about your job here?' The man had thrust a microphone under my chin and was smiling at me in a way that was supposed to be engaging, I guess. He didn't wait for me to answer the first question though, he just pressed on with the next. 'What it is that you do here? Dairymaid?'

I stepped into his personal space and pushed the microphone to one side. 'I don't work here.'

His smile held even as I pushed by him and on towards my car. 'Goodness.' He exclaimed, then, 'Come on, Bob.'

He ran to get ahead of me with his cameraman and tried again. Once more the microphone was thrust towards me. 'So, my lovely, if you don't work here, what brings you to this remote and foreboding farm? Are you another alien hunter, like me?'

This time I stopped. 'Look, I don't know who you are, and I have no desire to find out. I'm here as a private investigator hired by the farmers and I am leaving.'

'Stop the camera, Bob.' Before I could get away his whole demeanour changed, and he hit me with a look that could only be described as soul-searching. It made me wonder if he practised it. 'I'm an investigator too.' He said softly. 'There are alien creatures visiting this place and I fear for the families. Will you help me?'

I had to pause and look at him. He sounded so sincere, so honest. He reached back to give Bob the microphone then extended his right hand to me. 'Jack Hammer.'

I had little option other than to reciprocate. Anything else would have been extremely rude. 'Amanda Harper.' We shook hands.

'Amanda Harper.' He repeated my name and kept hold of my hand. 'Amanda Harper.'

'Yes, Amanda Harper. Can I have my hand back now please?'

He turned his head slightly to speak over his shoulder but did not take his eyes from mine. 'Bob where do I know her name from?'

'Works for Tempest Michaels.'

His eyes bulged at the news and his jaw hung slack. 'You're a paranormal investigator. Why didn't you say?'

'Nothing to tell.' I replied, wondering how it was that I had come onto their radar.

'Nothing to tell? You must be joking.' He finally let go of my hand and switched his demeanour yet again, this time to serious. 'Look, Amanda, I have been talking about having a co-host for my show for months now. You are the perfect fit for the role. You have credibility, you have presence.' He looked me up and down as if appraising me. 'I couldn't come up with a better sidekick. Oh, Bob this is wonderful. Isn't this wonderful, Bob?'

'S'pose.' Bob said.

'I'm sorry, Mr Hammer. I already have a job.'

He barely even bumped from my rejection as he steamed straight towards signing contracts. 'This is the chance of a lifetime for you. Don't blow this off without giving it some consideration. We had over two hundred thousand viewers last year.'

Two-hundred thousand? Not exactly a phenomenon.

'I need to go.'

'Really? You're turning this down?' I wondered if he meant the show or himself. 'I could make you a star!' I slid into my car, but he grabbed the door before I could close it. 'Come on, darling. Your chest alone would get me an extra million viewers.'

I slammed the door shut, almost taking his head with it, then quite deliberately spun my wheel as I gunned the Mini's engine to create a spray of cow shit that shot out the back of my car to pelt him as I escaped down the road and into the dark.

Whoever the figure by the milking shed was, there was no chance of speaking with them now. They would have to find me again later.

Once home, I had emailed James to see what he had discovered, chopped some peppers and onions to make a stir fry for my dinner and elected to take a bath. The bath was the lazy option. I was supposed to be going to the gym since I had not bothered with it this morning, but I really didn't feel like it. I would go for a run in the morning. A good sleep would make me feel more motivated. Right now, I wanted to eat ice-cream on the sofa watching Ryan Gosling movies while telling myself I wasn't going to get left on the shelf. Seeing the yummy farmer and his pregnant wife had reminded of what was missing from my own life. I was twenty-nine and single. My most recent boyfriend had lasted no more than a handful of dates before fate threw a spanner in the works. But Brett had been the real thing for a few moments and that bothered me more than anything else.

Later, floating peacefully in the bath, I remembered I was supposed to call my mum. I had meant to call her a week ago. She was a worrier and I loved her, but she thought I was still a little girl and not able to take care of myself. It drove me nuts. A week ago, I was going to call to tell her about quitting the police force. She didn't like that I had chosen a career in uniform and had constantly sniped at it over the years. It didn't pay enough, it was unbecoming of a lady, I would never find a man if I kept arresting them. The last point had been tinged with irony a week ago as the man I was dating at that point was one I had arrested a week earlier. Brett Barker, a millionaire with a hot body and perfect manners.

Had I called then, I would have been able to deflect her questions about my new job with information about my boyfriend. It would have worked too, but now I would just have to suck it up.

After my bath, I was cooling down while wrapped inside a huge cotton towel. Another towel adorned my head and I had big socks on my feet to ensure they stayed warm. I would cook dinner after the call.

With a little resignation, I sat down and picked up my phone. I didn't particularly want to, but I had news that she would complain I hadn't shared with her if I left it until she returned. She would also complain that

I hadn't called her enough, despite the fact that she was on a cruise ship and thus could be anywhere and I had no idea what she was doing at any point, while she could reliably predict that her spinster daughter would be at home every evening unless I was working a shift. Now she knew I had quit the police though and would have a stack of questions to ask.

I settled into the corner of the sofa with my legs tucked under me and the phone on my lap. It was on speaker, leaving my hands free to cradle the hot cup of coffee I had just made.

What time was it on east coast America? Were we four hours ahead or five? Or was it more than that? I could never remember but it was late evening here so I felt sure it was late afternoon wherever she was.

'Hello?' Mum's voice came onto the phone. She seemed surprised to have received a call and as if she was now wondering who it was even though I knew she had caller ID.

'Hi, Mum. It's Amanda.'

'Oh, hello, Mandy.' I hated when anyone called me Mandy. Only my mother got away with it. 'How are you? Why the call?'

Had she had a stroke? Had I imagined this afternoon's conversation?

'We spoke just a couple of hours ago, mum. I told you I quit the police service. You thought I was a prostitute. Does that not ring any bells?'

'Oh, yes. Yes, so you are not with the police anymore then?'

She sounded distracted. There was music playing in the background, something from the eighties.

'No, mum. I work as a private investigator now. I investigate my own cases and bill my clients for the hours I work.'

'That's nice, dear.'

That's nice, dear?

'We specialise in paranormal cases, ones with an unexplained element or where the client believes they have a paranormal problem.'

'How interesting.'

I could swear she wasn't taking in anything I said. 'The case I am investigating now involves aliens tampering with cows.' All I got to that revelation was quiet at the end of the phone. I changed tack. 'How's your holiday going?'

'Oh, well it's lovely, darling. I should have done this years ago.' At least that got you talking, I thought to myself. 'John always takes such good care of me. We had dinner with the Captain just last night. I have eaten so much lobster on this trip. More in the last month than the previous fifty years.'

'That sounds nice, mum.' I let her prattle on for a while. She had lots to tell me about where they had been and what they had done and about how John was the on-board Quoits champion. I didn't know what Quoits was, but I also didn't ask for fear she might explain it.

Suddenly, she sensed that she had been speaking uninterrupted for many minutes. 'Goodness, listen to me go on. How are you, dear? What are you up to? Is there a new man in your life?' I was exasperated that she was asking me questions when I had been trying to tell her the answers already. Her last question though was dragged out to demonstrate her hope that the answer might be positive.

I figured I might as well just talk to her about what she wanted to talk about. 'No new man, I'm afraid, mum.'

No reply.

I could hear her giggling at something, her voice muffled like she was putting her hand over the phone. 'Well, I did have a boyfriend briefly, but he saw me with someone else so dumped me and went to Coast Rica and I was kidnapped last week and stripped naked so I could be sacrificed by a voodoo priest.'

More silence and I worried that I had stunned her. 'Sorry, dear.' Mum finally said, 'I wasn't listening. John just went by on his way to the shower and I got distracted. What were you saying?'

FFS. She was too busy ogling her boyfriend's bum to even hear my shocking news.

'I said I got kidnapped and almost murdered.'

'That's nice, dear.'

'Mum, are you listening to anything I say?'

'What's that, darling? Sorry, John is dancing for me now. I have to go.' Just as the phone went dead, I heard her squeal with excitement. My mum's sex life was better than mine. Surely, that can't be right.

I gave the phone an accusing stare and felt my arm twitch with a desire to throw it at a wall.

Bollocks to it!

I was going to order take-out and drink a bottle of wine. There was a cold one in my fridge right now which suddenly had a limited life expectancy.

I rose from the sofa and stomped across my small apartment to find it. However, my doorbell rang before I got my hand on the fridge door and though I twitched with indecision, I went to answer it anyway.

I live in a safe apartment block in a safe part of town. I'm no fool though, so I put the safety chain on before I opened the door and peeked around it to see who was outside.

Not the Evening I had Planned. Wednesday, November 9th 1937hrs

Outside my door, with a massive bunch of flowers in one hand and a bottle of champagne in the other was the only person in the world I wanted to see right now.

Outside my door was Brett Barker.

And he looked hopeful.

Neither one of us said anything for a second, then I was slamming the door shut so I could get the safety chain off and he was starting to speak.

'Amanda, I'm so sorry. I made such a mistake.'

'Shut up.' I demanded as I threw myself at him. Then he couldn't talk because we were kissing, and I was so overwhelmed with happiness that I thought I might cry. He didn't know what to do with his hands as they were both full and he couldn't put anything down.

He broke the kiss as I dragged him into my apartment and kicked the door shut. I snatched the champagne from his unresisting grip and dropped it on the sofa as we stepped around it, still mostly locked at the lips. The flowers... I don't actually know what happened to the flowers but neither they nor my towels were still with us when we got to my bedroom door and tumbled through it.

I woke to the sound of Brett snoring lightly next to me. My bed wasn't big enough that we could share it and not touch each other so even though he was laying on his back on the other side of the bed, he was still partially intertwined with me.

I didn't move. I just stayed where I was, watching him sleep and breathing in the scent of him. I felt glorious. I felt victorious.

I felt horny.

The realisation that I felt a desire for physical affection and could instantly do something about it made my tummy go swirly for a second. Not that I hadn't got my fill last night. I just wanted more. He was like candy, only this candy wouldn't make me fat.

I gently eased back the duvet to reveal his toned torso. He was every bit as fabulous as I remembered. I didn't want to wake him, but maybe if I accidentally caused him to come awake...

I tugged the duvet a little more. What I wanted to see was just a few inches further south.

Mmmm inches.

'Find something you like?' He asked, his husky voice dripping with passion.

I bit my bottom lip as I locked eyes with him. Then he moved with sudden speed, flipping me onto my back and pinning me in place.

The rest, if you will allow me to paraphrase, was ecstasy.

Forty minutes later I was in the shower, getting clean and trying to think about work when the shower door opened behind me and it all started again. This time vertically instead of horizontally.

When I finally got to work a few minutes before nine o'clock, my legs were wobbly, and I was starving because I had missed dinner completely and only grabbed a banana for breakfast. I needed to check in with James, since I hadn't even looked at my emails since last night and I needed to find food.

And coffee. Definitely coffee.

Before I had left the apartment, or more accurately, before I let Brett leave, I had asked him how it was that he had come to believe I had not been cheating. He seemed reluctant to tell me the whole picture but said that he had come by information that proved he had been a fool. He distracted me with more kisses. Kisses that were heating up again and which caused me to insist he go before we were naked once more.

Driving to work, I thought about how Brett could have come to know I was not cheating on him. The answer I kept coming back to, was that Tempest or Big Ben had contacted him. Tempest seemed the more likely of the two to perpetrate the crime and he and Brett were not friends, so it felt right that Brett would be more inclined to believe him. Who else could it have been? A better question was whether I should be angry about it or not. I needed to think about that.

I found James in the office already, the dim November dawn light just starting to brighten the office naturally from outside while he sat under the bright white LED lights inside. He looked up as I crossed the office.

'Where do you get your eyeshadow?' I asked. James had been dressed as a girl more often than not since I met him but, on the occasions that he turned up as a boy, he never wore make-up. Until this week, that is. I suspected it was something to do with the events of last week when he had also been kidnapped and was to be ritually murdered. They hadn't spotted that he was a man beneath the dress and blonde wig until they stripped him naked. Now he came to work as a boy with boy hair and a full face of make-up.

Thing is, he wore it better than me.

'It's Mac.' He replied. That explained a lot. I couldn't afford Mac. A little voice on my right shoulder whispered that I had a multi-millionaire boyfriend again so could have whatever I wanted probably.

I shushed the voice while secretly smiling to myself.

'Are you okay?' James asked. 'You seem... different.'

I smiled again but said nothing.

Suddenly a Dachshund appeared by my feet. Then another. Both wagging their tails like mad and jumping up at my legs. Tempest had the cutest dogs I had ever met, I couldn't resist crouching to pet them. To me, they looked very similar although Tempest claimed he could tell them apart just by listening to them breathe. I had to check the tag on the little dog's collar to work out that I had Dozer's belly under my fingernails. The moment I reached for him, he had flipped onto his back for a tummy tickle.

'Good morning.' Called out Tempest as he came into the room after the dogs.

James answered with his usual, 'Hey, boss.'

I stayed where I was, stroking his dog for a few more seconds but smiled and said good morning in return. Then I remembered that I wanted to ask him about Brett. 'Have you got a moment?'

'Of course.'

Tempest was taking off his jacket and walking to his office when he replied. I gave the dog a final pat and left him with James. Ahead of me, Tempest had gone into my office and was looking out the back window at the late Autumn weather outside.

I opened my mouth to ask him the question that was bothering me but couldn't work out how to frame it. 'Um.' I managed.

'Alright. Out with it. What did I do?' His cheeks were colouring with embarrassment, I couldn't guess what he thought I was about to say but he had snapped out the demand with worried impatience.

It caught me off guard, but it did make me speak. 'Wow. Okay. Did you call Brett?'

His shoulders slumped. It looked like an act of guilty admission. 'Not exactly.' He turned away from me and scratched his head, 'Essentially though, yes. Please accept my apologies if I overstepped. I felt there was a wrong to make right.'

Okay, so I was right, and I had my boss to thank for my renewed relationship with Brett (and the fact that my legs felt like jelly). 'I would not normally tolerate interference in my relationships, but this time I feel I need to thank you.'

Tempest caught me smiling and took my right hand in both of his. He had something he wanted to say. His eyes were boring into mine, he looked nervous. Oh, God! Was he finally going to admit how he felt about me? It was a day too late if he was.

He opened his mouth to speak. Closed it again, gave himself a second and tried once more.

'Anyone for coffee?' James yelled from the front of the office.

Oh, thank God.

'Cor, yeah. I'm exhausted.' I called back, thankful that I could deflect whatever it was Tempest had to say, but certain it was going to be about his feelings for me. It seemed cruel, but I added, 'I didn't get much sleep last night.' So that Tempest would better understand he had missed his chance. I didn't want to have the conversation with him if I could avoid it.

He was still holding my hand. I knew he wouldn't voice his feelings now but I had to prompt him to speak nevertheless. 'Was there something you wanted to say?' I asked.

He gave my hand a final squeeze. 'Just that I am happy for you. I am glad it worked out.'

'Me too.'

Tempest changed the subject. 'How did the crop circle case go?

I moved behind my desk to put some distance between us, 'I have a case, that's for sure. Three farmers have joined together to hire us before they go out of business. They signed the contract and paid an advance yesterday. I will be getting stuck into it today.'

James stuck his head through the office door next to me. He had his coat on ready to go outside. 'What's it to be?' We gave him our order for the coffee shop and Tempest handed over a crisp twenty pound note.

He was hanging around to hear about the case, so I pulled out a map I had bought at a gas station last night on the way home. I wanted to mark different features on it to give me a clearer picture of where different events had occurred – alien craft sightings, crop circles etcetera. It might not help, but I was sure it couldn't hurt. 'We need more maps. I bought this one yesterday as it shows the area of the farms in some detail.' It was an Ordnance Survey map of Cliffe Woods and the area around it. Having folded it out I needed a wall to put it on. 'Have we got any pins? Or some Blue-Tac?'

'Somewhere, yes.' He replied but what he found was a roll of Sellotape.

'So, the three farms are here, here and here.' I drew three circles on the map. 'And the crop circles have appeared in these fields.' I put some swirling circles on to represent them.

We both stared at the map. 'That's about it actually. I don't know any more yet.' I admitted. 'Oh, I forgot to mention. You might get a call from a TV show chap. I met him yesterday. He seemed to think I should know him and was doing his best to be charming while mostly making me want to vomit.'

'Sounds like a top bloke. Why will he be contacting me?'

'Well, he might not, but he is the star, his words not mine, of an internet show where they search for proof of extra-terrestrial life. It's called Alien Quest. He did tell me what channel it is on, but I wasn't really listening. Anyway, he is investigating the crop circles for his TV show and was at Brompton farm trying to do some filming.'

'How did you end up speaking to him?'

'He cornered me on my way back to my car. He thought maybe I worked at the farm and wanted to ask me some questions. Made a big show of telling me I should be on camera. As I said, he was trying to be charming. I should have lied and told him I did work there but had to go, instead I said I was investigating the crop circles myself and suddenly he was asking question after question. His cameraman somehow knew who I was and knew about you. He might never call. I just wanted to warn you, in case he did.'

Tempest fiddled with his phone. 'Jack Hammer?' He asked as he showed me the picture of the slimy TV show host.

'That's him. I have to believe that he changed his name too - Jack Hammer. He sounds like an adult film star.'

Tempest nodded his agreement.

The office door opened again as James came back through it bearing a tray of coffee cups and a bag that probably had a donut in it for him. My stomach growled meaningfully but Tempest had already left to get his hot brew and didn't hear it. I was going to need to get food really soon.

By ten o'clock, Tempest had already left for the day, pursuing a case that appeared to involve suburban witchcraft and I had gone for food. There was a shop a couple of doors along from us that made sandwiches fresh every day. I was hungry and had missed meals so grabbed the ultra-dirty chicken, bacon and stuffing sandwich with mayo that I always lusted after and never bought.

What can I say? I was feeling naughty. I bought a vegetable smoothie to wash it down because that would balance it out. That's how it works, right?

I had eaten the first of the two triangles before I got back to the office and could feel the demand for sustenance subsiding as I crossed the room. I still needed to catch up with James about the research he had been doing.

A voice stopped me short. 'Amanda?'

I turned toward the voice, my mouth full of half-chewed sandwich. I was certain before I saw the voice's owner that I knew who was behind me. There, framed in the office door, was my Uncle Knobhead.

'Uncle?'

'Hello, Amanda. So good to see you. It's your Uncle Knobhead.' Upon saying his name, James's head shot up to see what was going on.

'Wow!' said Uncle Knobhead, taking in James's makeup.

'Good morning.' Said James pleasantly before returning his attention to his computer screen.

My mother has an older brother called Norbert. As a child, I struggled to say his name correctly and it came out sounding close enough to Knobhead for the name to stick. Soon, everyone in the family called him that instead of Norbert. He hadn't shied away from it either, in fact, it would be more accurate to say that he embraced it as if he had finally found something remarkable about himself. He would actually regale people with the story, so it was not that great of a surprise that he was now announcing himself to the room as Uncle Knobhead.

He was grinning at me, the expression worrying. It made me think that he thought he knew something that I didn't know.

'Uncle.' I said again, this time in greeting as I swallowed my bite of sandwich and crossed the room to air kiss his cheek. I hadn't seen him in at least three years. 'What are you doing here? Please tell me you are not here with a case to solve.'

'No.' He said, his excitement brimming over. 'I'm here to help.' He came into the office fully now, closing the door behind him.

'Help how?' I asked, not sure I wanted to hear the answer.

'I got kidnapped by aliens.'

Right.

I just stared at him. Growing up, my Uncle had always been the fool that entertained me. At family gatherings, on the rare occasions when he visited our house or the even rarer ones when we went to his, he was always doing silly things. It wasn't until I reached adulthood that I came to understand that he *was* a fool. His life was mostly a mess of failed relationships, failed business enterprises and gambling debts that had culminated in a botched robbery and three years in jail. He was just that kind of a person. Now though I was waiting for the punchline.

Then it occurred to me that he couldn't know I was investigating aliens. Unless...

'My mother called you, didn't she?' She had been listening after all.

'She sent me an email.' He replied. He had wandered across to the small table in the seating area where we had tea and coffee facilities laid out. 'Are there any biscuits?' He asked hopefully.

'No, I don't think so.' I wanted to revisit the alien kidnap thing. 'When exactly, Uncle, did you get kidnapped by Aliens?'

Without needing to think he snapped out the answer, 'Saturday, May 13th, 1997.'

'Why have I never heard about this?'

'Oh, it's very hush hush. The government department that covers these things up made me sign a form to promise I would never speak about it.'

'But you are speaking about it.' I pointed out.

'Well, yes. Technically I am. But with you being *in the know* I don't think it counts.' He had given up on his quest for a biscuit and was helping himself to a coffee. There were sweeteners in a dispenser on the tray with everything else. He clicked the lid three times to dispense three tiny tablets then pocketed the dispenser instead of putting it back on the tray.

In the know?

I wasn't sure what he meant, but the safest thing I could do was not ask questions and get rid of him as swiftly and politely as possible.

'Your mum said I should volunteer my services. She said,' I watched his eyes go up as he scoured his memory for what she had written. 'Nobby you need to get yourself on the straight and narrow. Go and see Amanda and do something useful for once.' His eyes returned to horizontal and he looked at me like an eager puppy.

Ah, nuts! How was I supposed to turf him out now?

Just then the office door opened again. I had half a second of hope that it might be a customer and I would have to deal with them instead of my Uncle and might have time to formulate a plan to let him down gently. But no, I was denied. Coming through the door was Jack Hammer and Bob.

Bob was filming while Jack walked backward and talked to the camera.

'... and inside the office of the Blue Moon Investigation Agency, we find...'

'My word! Jack Hammer! As I live and breathe, it's Jack Hammer.' Exclaimed Uncle Knobhead, his excitement overflowing.

His outburst interrupted the flow of Jack's nonsense, but he recovered instantly when he saw that he had run into a fan. Jack was giving the room his best smile.

'Oh, what a great day this is turning out to be.' Uncle Knobhead had crossed the room, still holding his coffee which spilled on the carpet as he pumped Jack's hand for all it was worth. 'Your show is the best thing on the internet.'

Jack's smile, if possible, got even broader. Then he looked at me and said, 'Fans everywhere, Amanda. I bet this gentleman knows his fact from fiction.'

'Indeed, I do, sir,' said Uncle Knobhead. 'I'm one of those in the know.' He tapped his nose to indicate that he knew secret things and winked.

Jack was lapping it up.

I was bored. 'Mr. Hammer...'

'Jack, please,' he insisted.

I started again. 'Mr. Hammer. Is there something I can help you with?' I had a case to investigate and didn't need any of the daft distractions I was currently suffering.

'I've decided to team up with you. We can investigate this together. Together we will make the perfect pairing and when we find the proof we need, we can get the publicity that will send our show into orbit.'

'Oh. My. God,' Uncle Knobhead squeaked. 'Are you going to be on Alien Quest together?'

'Yes,' Jack replied.

'No!' I snapped.

'Amanda we will be perfect together,' Jack insisted.

'I dare say you will,' encouraged Uncle Knobhead.

In my head, I was Force strangling them both like a Jedi knight.

'Alien Quest with Jack Hammer and Amanda Harper,' Jack said, sweeping his arm through the air like he was seeing the title and names on a billboard.

'And their assistant, Nobby,' Uncle Knobhead added hopefully.

'Who's Nobby?' asked Jack.

'This is my Uncle Norbert.' I indicated Uncle Knobhead with my arm. 'Now both of you, get out. I have a case to solve and you two dummies are doing nothing but slowing me down.' The ultra-high buzz I had come to work on from last night's explosive release of endorphins was no longer able to still my annoyance.

I placed my hands on my hips and stared at the pair of them, my eyes flaring. I felt a little guilty kicking my Uncle out, he looked like a lost puppy with nowhere to go. Jack, I would have happily kicked in the arse to make sure he got the message, but I refrained.

He took a step toward the door, then stopped. 'Is Tempest Michaels here?'

'On a case,' James answered.

Jack looked disappointed, but only for a moment as his boundless enthusiasm seemingly couldn't be dulled for long. 'Never mind. I'm sure I will catch him later.'

I took a threatening step forward. He just laughed and held up his hands. 'Come on, Nobby. Let us be away from this place and talk of alien encounters together.'

My Uncle Knobhead all but levitated in his excitement as he ran after the sleazy TV host.

When they were both gone, I turned back to James who had been watching the spectacle silently. Instead of speaking, he indicated with his head to my right. I tracked his gaze and found Bob still standing just inside the door where he had taken up position on his way in. He was still filming.

I inclined my head to the left a little.

Did he really want to try my patience?

He got the message, waved his hand in supplication and backed out the door.

'That was fun,' said James.

I didn't agree.

I was faced with options on which direction I took my investigation now. I needed to go back to the farms and see the cows and the equipment and in fact the milk for myself. I was going to get a sample of the milk and sweet-talk the crime labs guys at the station into analysing it for me. There were the two college kids that Kieron had mentioned – I thought they were worth a visit, plus I wanted to see the lights in the sky myself.

The question I was asking myself over again was, what could be causing the luminous milk?

I had not even the start of an answer.

I had spent the last couple of hours going over research with James. None of it was conclusive or even particularly helpful. There was a lot of forums where alien nuts discussed theory about what made crop circles appear. One leading theory was that it was a form of communication we were too primitive to understand.

James had found some articles in scientific journals where a couple of people with lots of letters after their names had chosen to approach the phenomenon seriously. One which caught my eye claimed the circles were the impressions left by spacecraft as they touched down to earth and another that it was nothing to do with aliens at all and was the earth trying to tell us that we were killing it.

All in all, there was a lot of government conspiracy and cover-up claims but nothing that pointed me in a helpful direction. I asked James to move onto trying to find out what might be making the milk glow and to investigate the finances of the farmers and their staff. The latter task was going to be the hard one, he assured me – finances were behind walls of security, so he would get a general impression at best.

I left him to it and drove back to Cliffe Woods. On the way, I called Kieron.

'Good afternoon, Amanda.' He answered.

'Kieron, hi. I will be arriving at the farm soon. I need to start talking to your farm workers. How many do you have?'

He didn't need to consider the answer. 'Less than we had last week. The alien thing has spooked some of them, but twelve here, and across the three farms there are thirty-one not including Glen, Richard, and I and the wives.'

Thirty-one. It was going to take a while to talk to them all. 'I asked for a fresh milk sample.' I reminded him.

'I have it waiting for you in the fridge. You didn't say how much so I have a pint, but you can have as much as you want. It is not much use to me at the moment.' His voice betrayed his irritation.

We disconnected just as I was arriving at his farm. With three farms to cover and no idea what I might find at any of them, I had simply driven back to the one I knew. I would start there and let the case lead me. Pulling on my parking brake, I was looking around to see if Jack Hammer was anywhere in sight. Thankfully, there was no sign of him.

In the boot of my car, was an old pair of wellies I hadn't worn in years. If I was going to be in this environment, I needed them, although I was shocked I had enough presence of mind to remember them with Brett in my house this morning.

As I stuffed my feet into them, the ancient rubber creaking and resisting as I did, I spotted a pair of lads in their twenties. They were leading cows from a barn to a field, the cows mostly following one another and not seeming to need much encouragement.

'Hey, guys.' I called as I approached them. 'Can I ask you a few questions?'

'Babe, you can ask me anything.' One said. Both were younger than me, maybe twenty-two or twenty-three and not much to look at. Neither one had styled their hair this morning, perhaps if the likelihood of getting cow shit in it was high, I wouldn't bother either, and both were a bit spotty and scrawny, but it didn't stop either one from coming on to me the moment I spoke to them.

'Yeah. I might have a couple of questions for you too.' The other said with a leering sneer.

I gave them a bored expression. 'Boys I am here at Kieron's request to investigate the luminous milk. Your boss expects you to answer my questions so let's not start with me having to teach you some manners, huh?'

Mentioning their boss had the desired effect. 'Sorry, Miss.' Said the first.

'Yeah, sorry, Miss.' Echoed his friend.

I forced my smile to return – I needed answers and wanted them to feel willing to give them. I indicated to some hay bales stacked a few feet away, 'Shall we sit?'

I was already moving, the two chaps followed, taking up positions next to each other and just across from me as if the hay bales were arranged around an invisible coffee table. 'I'm Amanda, can I take your names, please?'

They gave them willingly as Gavin Crawford and Anthony Daniels. They both watched as I noted their names in my book. Then I asked them what their job at the farm was.

It was Gavin that answered. 'We mostly move the cows around and look after their feed. Take them from the high field in the morning, move them to the pasture in the afternoon and back to the high field at night.' A few more questions filled in the picture of general farm labourer. I had never worked on a farm and had only visited a working farm perhaps twice in my entire life, both times in my capacity as a police officer. Quizzing Gavin and Anthony was just giving me a background picture of the daily routine.

From the corner of my eye, I caught sight of a person peering at me from the side of a grain silo. I think it is a grain silo anyway. Whatever it is, there was someone quite conspicuously trying to be inconspicuous by hiding behind it to look out. The person was wearing a dark hoody with the hood up to disguise their face. Was it the same person that had been trying to get my attention by the milking shed last night?

I turned my attention back to the boys, conscious that I had stopped talking and was looking away from them. 'Who do you report to? Who's your boss?' I asked next, wanting to understand the dynamics of farm relationships.

Again, it was Gavin that spoke. 'Mr. Fallon is the boss, him and Mr. Adongo and Mr. Tanner, I suppose, but it's Mr. McIntosh that tells us what to do.'

'Mr. McIntosh?' I asked as I wrote his name down.

I glanced across at the grain silo again. The person there beckoned with one hand and slipped back out of sight. Anthony had just said something that I hadn't been listening to. 'I'm sorry, can you say that again, please?'

'You met him yesterday.' Anthony supplied. 'Gordon McIntosh. Grumpy old bastard.'

'He's ex-military.' Gavin explained. 'But he still acts as if we are his soldiers to command.'

With perfect timing, the grumpy old bastard appeared. 'Oi, what's all this sitting around? Get back to work.' The two lads were immediately on their feet.

I turned to face the voice. 'Good afternoon, Gordon. These two gentlemen are helping me with my investigation. I won't keep them long.'

His ruddy face made no attempt to smile. 'You won't keep them at all, Miss. Back to work, you two.' He instructed.

I reached to grab Gavin's arm. 'Stay here, chaps, won't you please? Gordon may I have a word?'

I attempted to move Mr. McIntosh to one side for a quick chat. He clearly thought that the tasks he had for the boys to complete were too important to wait. I needed no more than a few minutes of their time and wanted to speak with Gordon next.

'Gordon, I need them for a few minutes, that's all. I am here at Mr. Fallon's request. Do we really need to involve him?' I was hedging that he would back down rather than argue with the boss, but I was wrong.

'I run this farm, Missy, not him. This farm and the other two. Those three clueless idiots and their wives couldn't get through a day without me, so I'll do what is necessary and everyone else, you most especially, can stay out of my way.' He folded out a meaty index finger. I thought he was going to poke me in the chest with it, but it stopped short of making contact with my clothes. 'You leave my boys alone and don't be snooping around the sheds sticking your nose in where it isn't wanted.'

He turned away from me. I was dismissed. 'You two, hop it.' He commanded. Gavin and Anthony scurried away, leaving me standing by myself in the farmyard as Gordon walked off, never once looking back.

I debated having a word with Kieron. He had assured me that all the staff would cooperate and answer my questions. They had a vested interest in seeing the farm thrive as much as the owners did. It felt too much like running to daddy though, I would fight my own battles and there was something about Gordon's attitude that... what? Something. My notebook was still in my hand. Gordon's attitude felt out of place unless he was hiding something. I made a mental note. Then I considered my next move. If Gordon was here, maybe I should go to one of the other farms where he was not.

Before I did that though, I wanted to see who was in the hoody and what they wanted. Gordon was no longer in sight, so I checked around to see if I was being watched, then walked across to the grain silo. There was no one there. I glanced around but there was no sign of my mystery figure.

Where he been standing just a few moments ago was a message written with a finger in the dirt on the silo wall.

Look at the University pictures.

What on earth did that mean? I took a photo of it with my phone.

Back at my car, my wellies went into a plastic bag and I left Brompton farm and the unpleasant Mr. McIntosh behind me as I drove to Richard's farm just a couple of miles away. On the map, it bordered Kieron's farm, but to get there I had to wend my way around the countryside, once again pulling in for tractors to pass.

Much like Brompton farm, there was a large sign just before the entrance that announced Wendle Farm. I had to wait in the road for a large tractor towing an evil-looking machine behind it to exit before I could continue toward the farm buildings.

My phone pinged with an incoming text as I parked my car.

On the screen, it said, "**Thinking of you x.**" It was from Brett. What would be an appropriate response? I considered my options:

- I love you, please put a baby in me. - Too soon for that one.
- My hoo-hah misses you, get over to my place. - Too overtly slutty.
- Oh, I haven't thought of you at all. - Too cool and not even slightly true.

In the end, I went with, "**Me too XXX**"

Richard's farm was arranged differently from Kieron's but, in essence, it all looked about the same. There were cow sheds and there was cow shit everywhere and it stank. Ahead of me was an ancient stone farmhouse, a large one that appeared to have been added to over the last century. Next to it was a more modern building, the double-glazed windows, and spotlessly-white, rendered façade showed how new it was.

Curious, I went to investigate. I am an investigator after all. As I neared the doors, two women came out. They were barely more than girls. They had on wellington boots, stark white overalls with a matching apron and a hair net. The open door carried a stink of cheese.

'Hello, ladies. Is this the dairy?' I asked. I wasn't aware that they made cheese or butter, or any other products. It made sense that they would though.

'Yes.' They both said at the same time.

'I thought there was no milk being produced. What are they working with in there?'

The two girls were in their teens, maybe as young as sixteen or seventeen. Working in a dairy they were devoid of makeup which made it easier to see the fresh youthfulness of their skin.

The taller, broader, least pleasant looking one of the two sneered at me, 'Who's asking?'

I didn't respond in kind. Instead, I kept my smile in place as I answered. 'I'm Amanda Harper. I'm here to investigate the problems the farmers have been having with their milk.'

It was the other girl that took up the reply, 'How can we help you?' She was barely over five feet tall and was very slight of build. I doubted she would tip the scales at much more than ninety pounds and had a pinched, narrow face and mousy, brown hair.

'As I said, I am here to investigate the recent events and the luminous milk that is threatening to bankrupt the farmers.' As soon as the words left my mouth and I saw the girls react, I knew I had revealed a confidence. Richard hadn't told his staff there were problems.

The two girls suddenly looked worried and I tried to recover my position. 'I'm sure that is an exaggeration.' I pressed quickly on. 'Can I ask your names?'

I recorded them as Gemma Pavely and Carmel Cooper. They worked in the dairy along with nine other women making cheese and butter and yoghurt. They had joined the team in the summer when they left school which made me right about their ages. They knew that the milk was being bought in at the moment and that there was something wrong with the milk the herds were producing but beyond that, they had taken little interest.

'There have been a few odd events recently, crop circles, lights appearing in the sky, and the milk turning luminous. Have you seen the lights?' I asked.

'Nah, I ain't seen nothing.' Replied Carmel, the larger girl, so fast that she hadn't had time to think. It reminded me of the criminal, delinquent youths I had to deal with as a police officer. They would deny any involvement with anything. Even when we had them on CCTV wearing the same outfit they were standing in, they would still deny it was them.

I swung my gaze to Gemma, she was hesitating. She had something to say but was wondering whether she should. 'Carmel, can I speak to the lady alone, please?'

Carmel's eyes flared. I sensed that she was not used to being dismissed by the smaller girl and maybe was more used to using her size to get her own way. With me standing next to her though, she simply pulled out a packet of cigarettes and stomped off.

'Moody cow.' Gemma muttered once Carmel was out of earshot.

'What have you seen, Gemma?' So far today I had not had much luck getting anything out of anyone.

She looked about, checking that no one was listening, then leaned in close so she could whisper to me. 'My boyfriend knows what is going on.' She watched my face, probably making sure I was taking in the gravity of the information she was giving me. 'I can take you to him. He will tell you everything you need to know.'

My heart rate sped up a little. Was it going to be this simple? Had someone seen or overheard the person responsible and could reveal the motivation behind the odd events?

'Does he work here?' I asked. She shook her head but didn't say anything. 'When can I see him?'

'Tonight. It won't be safe during daylight.' Her tone of voice made it clear that she believed there was danger involved. 'I'm sorry, I can't tell you any more now. I don't know who might be listening.'

I stood up straight and looked around. There wasn't a person in sight and we were miles from anywhere on a farm in the countryside. The nearest neighbour was at least a mile away.

Gemma wouldn't be budged though. Her lips were sealed until tonight and she would contact me later with instructions on where to meet. I gave her my card.

Inside the dairy, I could see other women, but before I could get to them, a mud-covered Series-Three Land Rover skidded to a halt behind me.

'Here, are you the lady hunting the aliens?' The voice came from the driver, a man in his late fifties with thick glasses and a thicker mustache. He wore a flat cap on his head and an ancient-looking Barbour wax jacket undone to reveal a hand-knitted woollen jumper beneath.

Rather than correct him, because I was investigating milk tampering, not hunting aliens, I said, 'Yes.'

He beamed a huge smile. 'I found a spacecraft landing site.' He announced proudly. 'Hop in.'

I turned to speak to Gemma, but she had already nipped back inside and was hurrying away.

I turned back to the man, he was now hanging out of the Land Rover, one muddy wellington boot on the dirt and one still in the car.

'My mother taught me not to get into cars with strange men.' He fell squarely into the strange category.

'Nothing strange about me, love.' This did nothing to modify my opinion.

'Tell me what you found please.'

'It will be better if I show you.'

'Perhaps, but I am not going to see it unless you convince me that I should. Maybe we should start with your name. I'm Amanda.'

The man pulled out a camera. An expensive digital one with a telephoto zoom lens thingy on the front. I was no good with cameras, so I didn't know what I was looking at, but it looked expensive.

'Oh, err. Fred Carter.' He said as if remembering himself. 'I came here to capture images of the lights. I arrived a few days ago and have been moving around to find the best spot.'

'Have you seen anything yet?' I asked.

'Oh yeah!' He replied with glee. 'The aliens are here quite often. I think it is a reconnaissance mission ahead of an invasion.' He was fiddling with the camera as he talked. 'Here it is.' He said, offering me the camera screen to look at. 'I was a British Army Officer for many years, their movements represent a typical tactic before a big offensive.' He claimed knowingly. 'Now that I have proof, the Ministry of Defence will have to listen to me.'

There were several pictures of a clearing in a wooded area. The grass in the clearing was scorched, a dozen equal sized circles evenly spaced to look exactly like something with twelve rocket engines had blasted off to the sky. I didn't know what to make of it, however, I was curious enough to want to see it for myself. It could be nothing, but it felt connected to everything else that was going on here.

He started speaking again as I handed the camera back. 'I found the site this morning. I have been trying to track the lights to see if they touch down anywhere. The Defence Secretary will want to know about their weapons, what they look like, whether they are armoured or have shields our weapons will not penetrate. I think the reason I have had so little luck

71

tracking them to a landing site until now is that they have cloaking technology. The lights we see are nothing more than ion particles from the fuel dissipating in our atmosphere.'

Okay. So, the chap with the moustache was bat-shit crazy. I still wanted to see the landing site for myself.

'I'll follow you.' I indicated my car.

He laughed. 'You won't get that anywhere near the site, love. It's cross country most of the way.' He was waiting for me to get in the car with him. It was not an appealing choice but if he planned to attack me, I had dealt with worse.

'Okay.' I conceded and went around to the passenger's door. Sliding in, I asked, 'How do you know about me?'

'It's all over the news. A lady was shot by an alien with a freeze gun last night and an alien was seen at Brompton farm. I went there earlier today because the Supernatural Times ran a story on it.'

The Supernatural Times?

'One of their reporters was there trying to get a story and she told me that there was a woman hired to investigate it all. I asked around and it wasn't all that hard to track you down.'

I had yelled to be let in yesterday. The reporter must have been in the crowd of space nutters trying to get in to see the footprint.

I didn't have to worry about making conversation with Fred while I was trapped in his car being taken into a wood because he wouldn't shut up. The journey took less than fifteen minutes but felt longer because we were going slow most of the way. He wasn't lying about it being cross country. He had the Land Rover in crawler gear half the way because the tracks were slick with mud after the recent heavy rain. He prattled on about alien invasion theories, about government conspiracy to cover up previous alien contact and how there was an entire branch of the Ministry of Defence that was dedicated to alien invasion preparedness.

'That was why they kicked me out of the Army, you know.' He said at one point, finally eliciting a response from me.

'What was?' I asked to fill the brief silence.

'I found out about BARF. BARF is the British Alien Response Force, a secret branch of the MOD that monitors and makes ready for repelling alien invasion when it comes. I tried to join them. Put in my papers six times and they kept writing back saying I had it wrong and there was no such branch. I couldn't understand why they wouldn't want me to join their ranks. I had an exemplary service record. I had deployed on numerous operational tours and I had combat experience. Instead, they said I was nuts and discharged me.' His tone turned bitter as he spat out the final few words.

As we drove through the woods, I could see bright colours ahead of me. It looked like vehicles I was seeing between the trees.

'Dammit.' Fred swore from the driver's seat.

Ten yards later I knew what he was getting upset about. There were others at the site already. Word had spread, or someone else had found it.

As we came into the clearing, there was a swarm of people. Jack Hammer, his cameraman Bob, and my Uncle Knobhead with the world's biggest grin plastered to his face were all directly ahead of us. Jack was filming already, but there was another film crew just setting up to our left and two more to the right, one of which was a local television news channel.

Fred was muttering about the evidence being ruined by *bloody amateurs* as he climbed out his side of the car. Jack had seen the car coming but even when he saw me, he didn't flinch from the flow of garbage he was spouting to the camera. He was in full presentation mode.

Uncle Knobhead also saw me, my presence distracting him from what he was supposed to be doing. He began to hurry across the clearing in my direction.

'Cut.' Yelled Jack. 'Norbert, I told you, you have to stay on your mark. The camera was just about to pan to bring you into the shot. Then we get to talk about your encounter with the aliens.' Jack sounded frustrated, an emotion often associated with my Uncle.

'Sorry, Jack.' My Uncle replied.

'Okay, let's take five. We have visitors it would seem and, dare I say, a fan?' The question was aimed at Fred who was advancing towards Jack with a determined gait.

'A fan? A fan of what?'

Jack didn't know what to make of the response as if it were implausible that Fred not know who he was.

'Look, never mind whatever nonsense you are doing here. This is an important military site and I must ask you to leave.' Fred cupped his hands around his mouth to make his voice heard. 'Everyone stop what you are doing. BARF will be here shortly to secure this site. You are contaminating the evidence they will need to help identify where the aliens will attack.'

There was a pause, then three different camera teams tried to get to him first, all shoving microphones in his face.

'No, no. You don't understand. You need to leave.' I could hear him getting ever more frustrated as the reporters tried to ask him questions.

'How did you find us? Uncle Knobhead asked me. He had completed his trek across the clearing to where I was inspecting the nearest of the scorch marks.

Without looking up, I indicated Fred. He was now arguing with the reporters about sovereign rights to any evidence found at the scene. I was certain they would soon determine that he was just mental and not of interest.

'Isn't this exciting?' Uncle asked. 'Real aliens and I am going to be on Alien Quest with Jack Hammer interviewing me.'

I decided the question was rhetorical and continued with what I was doing. The grass was burnt completely away, right down to the soil beneath and it formed a perfect circle. I wanted to measure it but had nothing with me that I could use. Tempest would have produced a tape measure from his bag, the thought causing a mental note to carry more stuff in future. I thought about what I did have in my pockets. The answer was nothing much, but a pack of disposable tissues allowed me to scrape up some soil and wrap it into a little pouch. I shoved the remaining tissues into my pocket and used the plastic wrapper they came in to stow the tissue containing the soil.

It smelled vaguely of petrol or something similar. I was going to get it analysed.

I stood up. Fred was arguing with the camera crews and trying to wrestle a tripod from the hands of a man twice his size. When he gave up and looked like he might try his luck with the gear a petite woman was holding instead, I intervened.

'Fred, I have seen enough. Please take me back to my car.'

He glowered at the reporters for a moment before allowing his gaze to flick down to meet my eyes. I smiled at him which was thankfully enough to erode his resolve. His shoulders slumped slightly, the excitement passing.

'You will all have your footage confiscated by BARF before the day is out. Mark my words.' He warned them all. No one paid him any attention.

'Would you not rather stay with us?' Asked Uncle Knobhead. 'Jack says this episode will be the best ever and will get more views than ever.' I glanced across to where my Uncle was stood. Next to him, but facing away to the distance, Jack was whispering instructions while pretending to be doing no such thing. It wouldn't have fooled a five-year-old. 'I bet the show would be even more popular with a...' he paused while listening to the next whispered line, 'an attractive female co-host.' Another pause. 'One that would give gravitas to the content and compliment the male host's magnetic personality.'

He lapsed into silence. Jack turned around so he was facing me now and hit with a smile full of teeth.

Good grief.

'Now, Fred.' I insisted.

Fred looked confused by my exchange with Uncle Knobhead but shrugged his shoulders and trudged back to the car behind me. As I got to the passenger's door, a glint in the foliage to my right caught my eye.

Fred was climbing into the car, so didn't see me wander off. The engine came on as I bent down to see what it was that I had seen. In the grass, mostly concealed, was an odd-looking piece of metal. Made from an alloy of some kind, the object was about seven inches long and round but bent twice along its length. It was perfectly smooth and had a bulbous knob at one end and tapered point at the other. About halfway along its length, a lug protruded with a small, perfectly round hole in it.

Whatever it was, it had not been there for long. I slipped it in my pocket and got into the car.

Fred continued to mutter and moan about civilians trampling his evidence all the way back to my car. He was driving direct to Whitehall to find the Defence Minister right now he assured me as I got out of his car.

I had a question, 'Fred, if I wanted to see the lights for myself, where would be the best place to go?'

That I had taken an interest instantly perked him up. He turned away and rooted around in the door bin to his right. Producing a map, he then did his best to flatten it out and fold it to show the bit he wanted.

'There is a raised piece of land here.' He said while pointing to the map. Sure enough, there were contour lines depicting a small hill. On the map, it was labelled as Hogget's Hill. 'From there, you can see all the way across the Thames Estuary to Essex on a clear night. If you want to see the lights, that's your best spot and you will find others there already. There is a stack of alien fanatics there every night, amateurs obviously.' He said proudly because he considered himself professional.

Professional nutter maybe.

'They are camping there and discussing ridiculous conspiracy theories. None of them know about BARF of course, but they will soon enough when the troops arrive to repel the invaders.'

I thanked him for his help, wished him luck and was glad to wave him goodbye.

The sun was setting, soon it would be fully dark. Atop the steel-sided barn ahead of me a floodlight mounted on the eaves cast light down to illuminate the yard. The farm was strangely quiet, and I realised that for the first time I could not hear any cows. On previous visits, there had always been a continuous background mooing. Now it was absent.

I still needed a milk sample. Kieron had sent it for testing already, the results undefined but I had to question what the Health Ministry might have checked for. Simon and Steven at the crime lab could tell me more about it and I would be able to interrogate their findings.

I knocked on the door of the Farmhouse. As I waited for the door to be answered, I checked my phone. I had a text message from James:

Will you get back here before I finish? I have turned up a few things of interest.

I would call him shortly. Before I could though, noises came from behind the farmhouse door, the sound of someone approaching. Without responding to James's question, I slipped the phone away. The door opened to reveal Kieron's wife, Lara.

Her belly looked fit to burst and she seemed unhappy or displeased or some other negative emotion as she stood in the doorway looking at me without speaking.

'Hi, we haven't been properly introduced.' I said as I smiled and put out my hand.

'You're Amanda Harper, the crappy fake detective that has fooled my idiot husband and is costing me money. I'm Lara and I don't like you.' She replied without taking my hand.

Righto.

I slowly lowered my hand. Her overt hostility didn't feel like it was genuinely aimed at me. She was angry about something else. Possibly she had been fighting with Kieron and I had offered a release point for her frustrations.

'I'm sorry you feel like that. Do you believe that there is nothing odd going on here? How do you think the milk is getting contaminated?'

Lara eyed me for a second, then turned her back on me. 'I already told you. There are aliens here. I saw one. It killed my friend, Tamara with a freeze gun.' She turned away with a final comment. 'I'll send Kieron out.' and she kicked the door shut in my face as she went. Her rudeness was surprising. I had to wonder what was motivating it.

A breeze blew across the yard, moving a few leaves around and making me cold. I was glad of the layers I had on today, they had kept me warm, and my feet were snug in my boots but my face and hands were cold.

I shoved my hands inside the sleeves of my coat to keep them warm. Thankfully, the door opened again a moment later and Kieron's far more pleasant face appeared.

'Hi, Amanda. Did Lara leave you outside?' He asked. He looked a little shocked at the concept but I was sure he already knew the answer.

I didn't have to respond, he ushered me inside where the warm air was ever so nice on my face.

'I just came for the milk sample.'

'Oh, yes. Well, come in for a moment while I fetch it from the fridge.' I followed him through the house to the kitchen/living area I had been in yesterday. Lara was there, but upon seeing me she turned and hurried through a door to vanish from sight. She had something to say as she went though, 'I told you to sell.' Echoed back through the doorway.

'Why does she want you to sell?' I asked.

'Farming is a tough but rewarding life. I don't think she expected it to be as hard as it is and I had to borrow a lot of money to set this place up. She has been questioning whether we ought to sell and do something else since I met her.'

'She married you though?'

'She did, but it was a whirlwind romance so she didn't get to see what farming was like and next thing we knew she was pregnant.' Somewhere, deeper in the house, a door slammed. Kieron sighed. 'Sorry about Lara. I don't know what is wrong with her recently.'

'It's fine.' I started saying.

'No, I think it is just the late stages of the pregnancy. She is uncomfortable and swollen, I get that, but it is one thing to take it out on me but she seems to be aiming her malice at everyone. The baby is due any day, it will be a relief to everyone, I'm sure. Honestly, I expected her to be happy. We were talking about kids from the first date. It was all she wanted and...' he tailed off.

'Go on.' I prompted.

His cheeks coloured. 'Well, she was very keen to get on with the process of getting pregnant. Let's put it that way.'

What I read from that was, she was ripping her knickers off minutes after meeting him but had then gone on to marry him so perhaps she just knew she had met the right man. I couldn't think of anything to say so I stayed quiet. He sighed again. 'Sorry, I'll get the milk.'

He went through the same door Lara had escaped through to return five seconds later holding a large mason jar full of white liquid. It looked like milk if I ignored the soft green glow coming from it.

I thanked him and reassured him that I would get to the bottom of the mystery. Leaving the farmhouse a few minutes later, I regretted the statement. I had no idea what was going on. Why would I tell him I was going to solve the case?

Sensing that I was wallowing in self-doubt, I called James.

His deep voice came on the line. 'Hi, Amanda.'

'Hey, James. What did you find?' I had left him looking into various angles on the case.

'I have prepared a report and emailed it to you. Have you not got it?'

'One moment.' I switched between apps on my phone to see the email with an attachment from James three from the top. 'I have it. Is it a long one?' James liked to include a lot of detail.

'Not really. There isn't much to find. You said you already searched for alien sightings in Kent and for crop circle explanations, well I think you found most of what there was to find. Kent is too boring for aliens to visit. Until now that is. Do you want to read the report or have me give you the highlights over the phone?'

'Highlights for now, please.'

'The crop circles were first reported in September. There was a small news feature on the local channel at the time because they had never been recorded in Kent before. Your report has a link to the YouTube film of it. You said there were two college kids poking around the farm asking questions at the time?'

'I did. Kieron couldn't remember their names. Lee and something.'

'Lee Davenport and Christian Rogers.' James supplied. 'They are art students at Greenwich College. I haven't been able to ascertain what their interest in the crop circles might have been. There seems to be no connection between their studies and the events at the farm.'

'I tried calling the mobile number for Lee already. He hung up on me and hasn't answered it since. Can you find an address for either of them? Or where I am likely to find them?'

'Shouldn't take long to get home addresses. They finished their undergraduate degrees in the summer and went straight onto a Master's program.'

I made a mental note to intercept them at school. 'Anything on the milk?'

'Not a thing. Not yet anyway. I did research what could cause it to glow but didn't get very far. I need more time on that one.'

'Okay. Thanks, James. I'll have a good read of the report later.' I thanked him again and disconnected.

The next item on my agenda was to see Steven and Simon at Maidstone Police Station. They would be waiting for me if I got there in time.

I slid into my car and damned near wet my knickers when I spotted the hooded figure sitting on my passenger's seat.

'What the hell, man?' I screeched.

I swore quietly as my pulse settled. 'You gave me such a fright. Can you take the hood off, so I can see who you are now?'

The hooded figure slowly shook its head. It was creeping me out that the person inside didn't speak. I assumed it was a man because of the size and shape but it might not be. Stuff not knowing though, I grabbed my phone and flipped it to torch mode.

Shining it inside the hood made my heart rate spike again though.

The face looking back at me was reptilian!

Involuntarily, I screamed.

It took a second, but my brain caught up: I was looking at a mask. I could see where it ended around the eyes. Green, lizard skin covered everything but the two orbs.

The hooded figure reached for the door handle to get out but removed an envelope from the hoody's front pouch first. The envelope went onto the dashboard held by a hand covered in the same prosthetic skin.

'Hey!' I called as the mystery guest opened the door and began to get out.

I clambered out my own side of the car intending to give chase. My mystery hoody person had run off into the dark and was gone once more though. Not a word exchanged. Using my police training, I recorded what I knew. Probably a man, around five feet eleven inches tall with an athletic build. The eyes were disguised by contact lenses that made the pupils also looks reptilian. It wasn't much to go on.

I snatched up the envelope. It wasn't sealed and there wasn't much inside, just a single piece of paper that appeared to be blank. It wasn't though, I was holding it the wrong way around. When I turned it over, I discovered a short sentence on the other side.

Check the soil

Another cryptic clue. I sighed inwardly and pressed the ignition button.

Finally, the message from Gemma came as I was driving back over the bridge from Strood to Rochester. She wanted to meet in the carpark of the Tesco supermarket in Strood at eight o'clock. It was a twenty-minute drive from my house, but it was easy enough to get to. Her message went on to explain that her boyfriend wanted somewhere public and lit but with good escape routes. He sounded more than a little paranoid.

Regardless of any misgivings, I replied to say that I would be there. I needed a break in this case. So far, I had nothing but weird. The spaceship landing site today, the luminous milk, the unfriendly farm workers. The mysterious person in the hoody and their enigmatic messages. Gemma's boyfriend knew something, or so she claimed, and that could get me looking in the right direction.

I was being hopeful.

The clock in my car told me the time was just after five o'clock. In my head, I was doing math to see how I could fit in a date with Brett. There would be time between getting home and going out again. We could do a late-night booty call, I was tempted to suggest it, but it felt too early in our relationship to be calling each other just for sex.

I called him anyway. I wanted to hear his voice.

The phone rang only twice before his velvet voice came on the line. 'Amanda, babe.' I could hear the smile in his voice. I was wearing one as well.

'Hi, Brett. How was your day?'

'After last night, nothing was going to dampen my day, babe. Although, I will say that I have been a little tired and wanted a nap this afternoon.' This made me giggle in a semi-embarrassed, semi-excited way. We really hadn't got a lot of sleep last night.

'It was a lot of fun. When do I get to see you again?'

'How about tonight?' He asked, his tone playful.

Now I wished I hadn't arranged to meet Gemma and her boyfriend. 'Maybe...' I dragged my answer out. 'I have some things I have to do tonight so I'm not sure what time I will get home. Not before nine, I expect.'

'Are we talking late night booty call, you naughty girl?' I could hear the excitement in his voice.

It did feel naughty. I couldn't recall ever having a booty call before, but if I was ever going to, I couldn't come up with a better partner than Brett. 'Yes.' I murmured into the phone breathlessly. 'Come whenever you want. I'll be waiting.' God, I was horny suddenly. What was he thinking right now? Was he picturing me naked?

He whispered into my ear, 'I'm going to make you beg for mercy, babe.' Then he was gone.

My legs felt weak.

Crime Scene Guys. Thursday, November 10th 1802hrs

I had called the number for the crime lab so they would know I was on my way. I was still working on favours and suspected that I would need to devise some way of paying them back soon. I think they dealt with my odd requests as a hobby more than anything else. They had no need to take the work on. Nevertheless, when Simon answered the phone, he was clearly pleased to hear my voice and asked what I had for him.

They were just about to finish work so were going to meet me in front of the station. His suggestion meant I could avoid going inside where I might run into CI Quinn.

At this time of day, parking was easy and I risked not paying for a ticket in the carpark just along the road from the station as I was only going to be a few minutes.

Both Steven and Simon were outside waiting for me. I had always got on well with the two older men. Each was somewhere around fifty and had more hair coming out of their ears than they had on their heads. Neither wore a hat to ward off the cold air but both had their hands in the pockets to keep them warm.

'Hi, guys.' I waved and smiled as I approached.

'Hey, Amanda.' Simon answered while Steven returned my wave. 'You have an alien artefact for us and some milk, yes?'

'I have an odd piece of metal that I hope you can analyse, and yes I have some milk.'

'What's the story?' Asked Simon as he took the six-inch-long piece of metal from me. 'Where did you find it?'

I answered the second question first. 'It was lying on the ground in a clearing in the woodland near Cliffe Woods. The clearing had burn marks on the grass where crazy people are claiming a spacecraft touched down. It didn't get there by itself.'

'It's really light.' Simon observed as he handed the odd component to Steven.

Steven hefted it in one hand and tried to scratch it with a fingernail. 'It might be a magnesium alloy?' He asked Simon.

'Easy enough to find out.' Simon replied. 'Tell us about the milk.'

I filled them in on the whole story of the farms and their cows and the crop circles and the lights in the sky at night and all the nutters it was attracting. While I was talking, I remembered the little tissue packet of burnt soil I had in my pocket.

'I also have this.' I said as I produced the plastic pack with a tissue inside it.

'You sneezed?' Steven asked, mystified.

I cocked an eyebrow at him. 'This is soil from one of the burn marks. It smells like petrol.'

Steven took it from me and sniffed it himself. 'Paraffin.' He concluded. 'Probably paraffin, anyway. It will be easy to work out. Not much extraterrestrial about paraffin, I'm afraid.'

I nodded. The chaps were clearly on their way home. Finished for the day but always on call if they were needed somewhere. 'How soon do you think you can look at this?' I asked cagily. I needed it now, or at least very soon. I couldn't say that to two fellows doing me another massive favour though.

Steven hefted the odd metal component again looking thoughtful. He glanced at Simon. 'Probably tomorrow?' He asked.

Simon nodded. 'Yeah, probably tomorrow. It won't take long to identify the accelerant in the soil or what material this is.' He said holding up the metal thing. 'What it was used for or what it was originally fitted to might take a bit more work.'

'I can test the milk.' Steven added.

'There is going to be a cost this time though.' Simon said, his tone suddenly serious.

'We can't keep doing this stuff for free, you know.' Added Steven.

I was taken a little off guard. My normally friendly crime-scene guys were suddenly bordering on aggressive and were both looking down at me with rigid expressions.

'Err, okay.' I managed.

'We would like...' Steven started.

'We demand.' Cut in Simon.

'That's right. We demand... A box of donuts.'

I relaxed, my shoulders slumping where I had been tensing. With a chuckle, I said, 'The best donuts I can find. I promise.'

'Super.' They replied simultaneously.

We chatted very briefly about work because they asked me how I was settling in at my new job, but I sent them on their way soon enough. They both had wives and children to get home to.

Satisfied that I would get some answers from their endeavours in a day or so, I walked back to my car.

Where I found a fixed-penalty-notice stuck to the driver's window. I snapped my arm out to check my watch.

Twelve minutes.

Twelve friggin minutes! I ripped the fine open. A fixed penalty for failing to display a parking ticket. I cursed myself and was thankful the rotten parking attendant wasn't in sight still as I might just vent my anger at them.

My watch told me it was a quarter after six. I was going out again in ninety minutes and I needed to eat and sit my backside down for a while, but Brett was coming so I needed to straighten the apartment and put on fresh bed linen. It was turning into a long day, but it had a promising ending. I just hoped Gemma's mysterious paranoid boyfriend had something great to tell me. I really didn't want to go, I wanted to stay at home and get ready for Brett.

Inside my apartment, I ripped the top off a microwave rice thing and gave it ninety seconds of nuclear heat. I needed to eat. I needed to tidy and make ready for a visitor and I needed to look at the research James had sent me.

While the microwave whirred, I ran through the apartment, turning on my laptop, stripping the bed and shoving things into the dishwasher. As the ping sounded to say the rice was ready, I was stuffing dirty bed linen into the washing machine.

I dumped the rice onto a pack of prawns and added some salad leaves from the fridge. Hardly a feast but it was what I had time for and would keep me going.

With a fork in one hand and the steaming bowl in the other, I sat cross-legged on the sofa in front of my laptop and clicked to get the research file open. James had pulled together a file that ran to six gigabytes. For a moment I worried it was going to be like trying to read an encyclopaedia but saw that the file contained videos and photographs which took up most of the space.

It was broken down into sections which allowed me to quickly skip the part on aliens in Kent and crop circle theories. I had read about them already. Mostly, I wanted to look up information on the people involved i.e. everyone that worked at the farm.

I started with the deceased, Tamara Mwangi. Also Kenyan, she was forty-three years old at the time of her death and had worked in the pharmaceutical industry for most of her life. There was a LinkedIn profile to show who she had worked for. James had pulled together a life history but skim-reading it, none of it meant anything at this stage.

Then I looked at Kieron and Richard because the hooded figure had told me to check the university photograph. As I opened their file, I wondered if I would find that the story they told about meeting at university would prove to be a lie. It wasn't though, James had found their graduation photographs on social media and they had indeed studied agriculture at Cambridge. They were bright guys. Wading through the reams of information, I came across a picture of the two of them in a class photo. They were sitting next to each other in the front row. Apart from having different hairstyles, they looked the same. Quite what the hooded figure expected me to learn I couldn't tell.

I was shutting the lid of the laptop when I saw another photograph labelled Dorchester University. I clicked on it, expecting to find another picture of the two men, but it wasn't them in the picture. It was Lara and Michelle. It was five years ago, and they looked no different from now. Kieron and Richard said they met them in a bar when the two girls walked in together and sat down next to them. The girls had to know each other from somewhere, the somewhere turned out to be university.

I checked my watch. I needed to get on with other tasks.

I arrived a few minutes early to find a parking space. My paranoia was telling me that Gemma and her boyfriend were not going to turn up, that she had overstated what he knew and I was wasting my time. Because of that, I had written a shopping list before I left the house and was planning to quickly do my weekly shopping if she wasn't here.

Sitting in my car, I called the number she had messaged me on earlier. It connected immediately.

'Hello, is that Amanda?' A man's voice asked. The voice sounded young, which I expected given Gemma's age and it had the awful guttural accent that many parts of the Medway Towns bred. I had no doubt he would drop every H and T and use swear words as punctuation in even the briefest sentence.

Was it better to make myself sound like him? Would he feel more relaxed and ready to talk than if I countered his accent by making myself sound like I came from Royal Tonbridge Wells?

I went with option one. 'Yeah, dis is 'Manda.'

'What's wrong with your voice?' asked Gemma. He had me on speaker, possibly through the in-car system.

I felt my cheeks redden as I said, 'Nothing.' In my usual voice. 'Can we meet in person?' I asked. Surely having dragged me to a supermarket car park there was no need to hide in our cars. If we were going to do this over the phone, I could have been at home.

'Yeah.' The man's voice returned. 'I just needed to make sure you were alone.' More mystery.

My car engine was already off, the phone to my ear, so I climbed out of my car and stood up. 'Can you see me?'

A set of headlights flashed on a battered looking Mitsubishi Eclipse a row over from me. Then the car's interior illuminated as the door opened to show me Gemma and her boyfriend. The tiny Gemma had found herself an equally small boyfriend. He looked childlike in his proportions and had left the thin wisps of hair growing above his top lip and across his chin in a bid to make himself look older.

I walked towards them, but he grabbed Gemma's arm and pulled her towards a darkened corner of the carpark. He made sure I saw and nodded with his head that I should follow them.

'Have you got any recording equipment with you?' He asked before I could introduce myself.

'No.' I answered. He was looking me up and down but not in a leering way, he was checking to see what I had on me, to see if I had a hidden camera in a coat button, what was in my hands etcetera. He was a nervous little mouse, his movements jerky and sudden.

'You need to put your bag over there.' He insisted, pointing to a forlorn-looking shopping trolley with three wheels. 'And empty your pockets.'

I hesitated, convinced that none of his nonsense was necessary. I was already here though, and I had come this far with his rubbish, I might as well play along a little further.

When I had shown him my empty pockets by turning them inside out and he was convinced I wasn't wearing a wire, he finally relaxed.

'Now are you ready to talk?' I asked while trying to keep the irritation from my voice.

'That depends, lady. Are you ready to listen?' He eyed me knowingly like he was the one with all the answers. I was getting impatient. Perhaps sensing my attitude, he pressed on. 'What I mean is, most people are not ready to hear the truth. It's scary for most folks to hear.'

Okay, I was officially bored. I took a step toward him. I was at least six inches taller than him. 'Start talking, little man, please. So, I don't have to hurt you.'

He took a quick step back, putting a protective arm across Gemma to shield her from the angry blonde woman 'Okay, love. Keep your hair on.'

'Tell me something interesting. Do it now.'

'It's the cows.' He whispered, his voice so quiet I was forced to bend and lean in to hear him. 'They have been bringing cattle from their home planet to impregnate our cows.'

Oh brother.

'Gemma is working there as a spy, risking her life to expose the truth.' He gave her hand a squeeze. 'Their plan is to seed the world with their superior genetic code. Through their breeding program they will develop superior creatures that will obey their instructions and when their numbers are a match for ours, they will strike. No one will see it coming and because we will have been eating their modified livestock, we ourselves will be unable to resist their commands. That is why Gemma and I are vegan. Only true vegans can survive the coming apocalypse.'

Gemma saw the look on my face. 'You have to believe him.' She begged. 'I have infiltrated the farm unnoticed. The farmers are all in on it. The aliens must have promised them that they would be spared or that they would be granted seats of power under the new order. I can't stop them by myself. Will you help us?'

Wowza, these guys were full crazy. 'Look,' I started. Then stopped because they were both looking beyond me at something else.

'Who did you tell about this?' Gemma's boyfriend screeched. 'You set us up.' He was trying to pull his jacket over his head to hide.

I spun around to see what had spooked them. Behind me, Uncle Knobhead and Jack were walking towards me with Bob filming everything.

'I thought I could trust you.' Wailed Gemma.

Ignoring the two teenage nutters, I crossed my arms and gave the two men a hard stare. 'I'm going to guess that your presence here is not a coincidence, so have you bugged my car, or are you tracking my phone?'

Jack was talking to the camera as usual, '… new Alien Quest co-host Amanda Harper is meeting with two victims of the alien activities here in Kent. Let's hear what information she was able to obtain from them. Will it help us track the aliens to their base on earth? Will we be able to stop the invasion together? Heed me Alien Questers: We will need your help soon.'

He had closed the distance to me, his annoying smile revealing perfect whitened teeth as he pushed the microphone he held under my nose. Bob stepped back and to the left to make sure we were both in shot and my Uncle, grinning like an idiot, waved to the camera.

'We're live, Amanda. Tell your audience what you learned tonight.'

'We're live?' I asked.

'Yes,' he said, turning his face to the camera. 'Right now, millions of viewers are seeing you for the first time.'

'And me.' Added Uncle Knobhead.

Jack ignored him. 'They want to know if they can sleep safely in their beds tonight. Are the aliens coming? Or are they already here?'

'We're streaming live right now?' I confirmed.

'That's right.'

I kicked him in the nuts.

He folded in half, dropped the microphone, cupped his groin and slowly collapsed to the ground while groaning. It was assault. I doubted he would be pressing charges though.

I turned to the camera. 'If there really is anyone dumb enough to be watching this rubbish, go and find something to do with your life. There are no aliens. There never has been. Put on some clothes, leave the house and go meet someone, a friend, a relative, just get out and have a life.' I gave a tiny bow and turned back to look at my uncle.

95

'That was solid gold.' Bob said breathlessly behind me. 'Our best show yet.'

Uncle Knobhead was dumbstruck, his eyes switching wildly between me, Jack, and the camera Bob was still holding.

'How did you find me?' I demanded

I guess he saw that I meant business because he ratted his new best friend Jack out in a heartbeat. 'He had me put a tracker on your car.' He blurted while pointing at the prone figure.

I took a step towards Jack. 'Why?'

'I needed to know where you were going. This is a great story.' Jack managed to grunt out. 'Just don't kick me again, okay?'

'Where is it.' I hissed at my Uncle.

'On the roof by the GPS aerial thing.'

I walked over to my car where, sure enough, there was a small, silver thing about the size and shape of a bottle cap stuck to the roof of my car. I might never have noticed it. It came away when I levered a fingernail beneath it. I carried it back to them.

'Any more of these?' I asked. 'Another one fitted as back up?'

'Nope.' Jack said. 'Look, I just wanted to join forces with you. You are a natural for the camera. Together we could have millions of viewers and you are already a paranormal detective. It's a perfect match.'

'I said no already.'

'I can't take no for an answer.' He was beginning to get up.

'How very rapey of you.' I snapped. 'I'm leaving. Don't follow me.'

Gemma and her boyfriend had scurried back to his car. A squeal of tyres heralded their departure from the supermarket carpark. It had been a wasted evening. One I could have spent with Brett doing things that would have been far more interesting. That was still going to happen, but I had to stifle a yawn when I thought about it. I had been going for hours already. I was going into the supermarket to get a can of something filled with sugar and caffeine.

'Amanda.' My Uncle was calling my name and running after me. 'Amanda.'

I slowed my pace and turned to give him a mouthful.

'I'm sorry, love. I was just trying to be helpful. I always get it wrong.' I wanted to shout at him, but it still felt like kicking a puppy. He was just so crap and useless and had been getting it wrong his entire life.

I opened my mouth but couldn't work out what I wanted to say. He spoke for me. 'Uncle Knobhead. I couldn't think of a more apt name for myself. You're the only family I have, Amanda. You and your mother, and your mum doesn't really want to see me ever. If I could make a mess of it, I have done. Every relationship, every job, every opportunity. I might as well accept it and leave you be.' He had his daft pork pie hat in his hands and was turning it nervously, looking pathetic.

Whether he was deliberately trying to make me feel bad for him or not, it was working. I needed to say something positive to him, but the truth was that he was right. He had made a mess of his life.

'I thought I might be able to help Jack and maybe get a semi-regular spot on his show, because, you know, I was kidnapped by aliens and all. I thought it might finally be the break I have dreamed of. A chance to be someone.'

I hung my head. Then a thought occurred to me and I looked back up with a smile.

'How would you like to look for lights in the sky with me?'

He brightened instantly. 'Really?'

'Get in.'

My uncle jabbered like a chimpanzee as I drove back to Cliffe Woods again. I wasn't listening to what he was saying, he was babbling nonsense about alien conspiracy through the years, but I did pick up that he really knew the subject. He was full of facts about the Roswell crash site, meteor impacts, and alien encounters, about films on the subject and how some directors had clearly employed consultants who had been kidnapped because their depiction was so accurate.

I thought about Brett and what I should be doing with him tonight. I had called him from the car park to let him know I would be getting home later than planned. He asked if I wanted to postpone. I was trying not to yawn when he asked but I couldn't suppress it. Generous as always, he assured me it was fine to postpone, he had work in the morning too. Then he said some naughty things about what he planned to do to me that made butterflies flit around my tummy, promised to see me on Saturday instead and was gone.

While I daydreamed about his yummy body, next to me Uncle Knobhead kept on jabbering nonsense. I didn't interrupt him, it helped to pass the time as I tried to find the place Fred had said to go.

In the end, it was easy to tell we had found the right place because there were dozens of cars parked at the side of the road. Cliffe Woods is a flat expanse of land that is barely higher than the Thames Estuary it borders. There are lots and lots of lakes and very little contour, so the one hill that exists in the area had attracted all the alien watchers because it provided an elevated view from which to watch the sky.

As we neared the cars, someone jumped out at me, I caught a flash of an arm in my headlights, making me jump.

I jabbed the brake in reaction and the person tapped on my window.

'Turn your lights off.' The person insisted.

I complied, but now the darkness enveloped me. The unseen person tapped on the window again. I powered it down an inch.

'I'll guide you in. Just follow my light. Oh, hello again.' It was Fred. 'Found the place okay then?' He didn't wait for me to answer, instead, he vanished into the dark and turned on a flashlight with a red filter. It was almost the only thing I could see as I followed it a few yards further down the road. He was walking in front of me.

'What's all this about?' Asked Uncle Knobhead.

'The red light doesn't penetrate very far, and I am guessing they want everyone's lights off to maintain the darkness here. Away from the city, it is much darker, which gives a far better view of the sky.' Fortunately for me, I had practised using a red light for night manoeuvres while I was in the police. Only once or twice though and I was not a fan as it is so disorienting. I couldn't see anything right now and could be getting led into a bog for all I knew. Just when I felt my panic rising, the light shut off and the man appeared back at my window.

'Welcome.' Fred said through the glass of my window.

I grabbed my phone, killed the engine and opened my door. 'Let's go.'

Uncle Knobhead got out of his side and came around to join me.

'Follow me. They are already here.' Whispered Fred.

Who is? I wondered as I scrambled up the bank behind him. Then, as we breached the crest of the small hill, I saw what he was referring to. There were a pair of green lights in the sky.

We were looking out over the moonlit plains that led to the Thames, way off in the distance. Light coming through the clouds was reflecting off ponds and small lakes, making the landscape light enough to make out features. Not that there was anything to see – no houses or buildings or roads. The farms were behind me somewhere to the East, the land ahead was too boggy for agriculture.

No one was looking at the land though. The eyes of the hundred or so people present on the hillside around me were all glued to the green lights as they whizzed around in the sky.

My heart was thudding in my chest. What was I seeing?

Uncle Knobhead whispered a question into my ear. 'Still think there are no aliens?' I turned my face slightly to see him while also keeping an eye on the lights. 'The same thing was seen a few years ago in New Zealand.' He explained. 'The phenomenon went on for six weeks. They sent up light aircraft to get close to them, but each time they did, the lights just disappeared. In the few shots they were able to get, all you can see is the lights. Proof of cloaking technology. The leading theory regarding the lights is that they are the exhaust ports for their propulsion system and cannot be cloaked.'

'Why is there no noise?' I asked. It was eerily quiet if there were two alien spacecraft overhead.

'That one I cannot explain. I did read a NASA engineer's report on organic engines once though. He proposed that it would be possible to make an engine that had no clunky moving parts and would not burn a fossil fuel as we would need. Their technology must be so advanced that we don't even understand it.'

Mesmerised, I watched the lights perform a series of intricate spirals. They were almost dancing in the sky. Fifteen minutes later I was still watching them and hadn't spoken at any point. Then the pair of lights dropped vertically down to hug the ground. They were a mile or more away and at that low level, they were close enough to the foliage that they kept disappearing as branches obscured our view.

Then they were gone.

What had I just witnessed?

The crowd of people on the hill were beginning to move.

A voice appeared by my right ear. 'That will be all for tonight. They won't be back.' Said Fred. 'This is what we get most nights.'

'Are they here every night?' I asked

'No.' Fred replied. 'Tuesday and Thursdays mostly but they have been seen at other times.'

'Tuesdays and Thursdays?'

'That's right.'

'Doesn't that seem awfully specific?'

'They're aliens, love. We are supposed to struggle to understand them. There is probably a code embedded in their movements that is being received by a mothership stationed outside our detection range.'

I needed to stop asking the crazy people questions. They always had answers.

I thanked him and bid him a good evening, then carefully made my way back down the hill to find my car.

After I dropped Uncle Knobhead off at his flat in the nearby village of Snodland, the question of what the lights were would keep me awake into the small hours.

Lights in the sky. If I told myself they were man-made I had to instantly ask myself how. The mystery was deepening and I was as clueless now as I had been two days ago.

I hadn't slept well and woke up tired. I rolled onto my back, warm and snug beneath the covers and told myself to get up. I had things to do. I needed to go for a run or go to the gym and I needed to get back on the stupid alien invasion case.

I was reluctant to move from where I was though, so I stayed there – *just a few more minutes* I told myself.

In my head, I ran through the case.

- The farmers were in financial trouble. That was what Kieron had told me and I had no reason to doubt it since they had hired me to save them from bankruptcy. James had thus far had little luck confirming their financial picture though.
- Kieron's wife wanted him to sell. Was she just sounding off? Or was that a genuine clue?
- Something was getting into the milk. The crime scene guys would work out what it was probably (need to remember to buy donuts). But the question to answer still was how it was getting into the cows.
- The strange lights in the sky were probably nothing to do with the case. Unless, of course, there really was an imminent alien invasion and the milk and crop circles were a part of the same problem.
- Then what about the landing site with the burnt circles in the grass?
- Kieron had an unusually stroppy wife. She was going to deliver the baby any day but there was still something about her attitude that didn't fit.
- Gordon the farm manager was horrible and arrogant and seemed convinced that he was the one in charge. He was up to something, but I couldn't tell what.
- There was a mysterious person in a hoody that was giving me cryptic clues that so far meant nothing.

Adding it all up just gave me a headache. I had to admit I had not a single lead. Then I remembered the two college kids and called the number I had for them again. I got the same response as usual when the person at the other end rejected the call once more. If I wanted to talk to them, I would have to seek them out. Locating them was a task I had already given to James.

Feeling a renewed determination to start eliminating some of the questions, I threw off my covers. It was cool in my flat, my naked skin suddenly goose-pimpling as I shuffled into a pair of fluffy mules to fetch my handbag.

As I left the bedroom, two faces turned to face me.

I screamed and leaped back through the door I had just left. 'What the hell are you doing in my apartment?' I yelled when the shock subsided.

I peeked around the doorframe. On the sofa, looking very sheepish were Jack Hammer and Uncle Knobhead. I had just shown them everything I had to show and the heat from my red cheeks was making me feel quite livid.

They still hadn't answered my question. 'What are you doing here?' I demanded with a lot more volume.

'Ack.' Said Uncle Knobhead. He cleared his dry throat and tried again. 'We have a new lead.' He tried, uncertain that this would justify being in my flat.

Jack looked less perturbed. 'A Polish lorry driver found the spacecraft last night. He took a video of it and the alien pilot and yours truly has the only copy. I aired some sneak peeks of it last night.' He claimed proudly. 'This way, the main reveal tonight will get many times more viewers.'

I fumbled for a dressing gown to cover myself up. Then, as I tied it around my waist, I stomped back into the living area. 'I don't give a...' I almost swore but caught myself. 'A hoot, what evidence you have. How did you get in here?'

Each got an accusing stare from me. I was used to interrogating suspects. These two would crack in no time.

Or I would hit them with something.

Uncle Knobhead looked the guiltier of the pair. I pierced him with laser eyes. 'I, ur. I learned a few tricks when I was less law-abiding than I am now.' He was struggling to meet my glare.

'Get out.' I hissed. When neither moved in the next nanosecond I repeated my instruction at a bellow.

'What about the video of the alien spaceship?' Jack asked as he scurried toward the door.

'Get out!'

Halfway out the door, he stuck his head back through. 'We'll wait outside then?' He didn't wait for an answer though as a picture frame was hurtling at his face. It hit the wall and stuck into the plasterboard for a moment before falling.

I fumed silently for a moment. Far too many people were seeing me naked recently. With the exception of Brett, which I was totally fine with, my boss, my best friend, the office assistant James, Big Ben, about fifty police officers, many of whom I knew and now my Uncle and the dickhead from the internet show had all got a good look at me.

It made me feel icky.

I went for a shower.

When I opened the door to my flat thirty minutes later, clean and dressed and telling myself I was ready for the day, I was struck by the smell of bacon. Jack and Uncle Knobhead were sitting on the tile of the landing with their backs to the wall and their legs jutting out. Each had the final bite of a breakfast sandwich from a local greasy spoon in their hands.

Jack started to get up. I waved him to stop. 'Stay there, Jack. I prefer you at my feet.' He did as instructed. 'How are your testicles?'

'Recovered, thank you very much.' He replied brightly. It seemed he wasn't holding a grudge for last night.

'Tell me about the supposed alien spaceship.'

'Not supposed, Amanda, love.' Uncle Knobhead clambered to his feet. 'Wait until you see it.'

'I'm going to the office. I will look at it there.' I was enjoying being in charge. I had forgiven Uncle Knobhead for putting a tracker on my car, but now he had messed it up again by breaking into my flat while I slept, rather than knock on the door as a sane person would. We would have a little chat about it later which he would not enjoy. I was going to make them dance to my tune for that matter. I needed nothing from them, but Jack and therefore by proxy, Uncle Knobhead, both believed they needed me.

I was already on my way down the stairs. 'Should we follow?' Uncle Knobhead asked, still standing on the landing.

'Come on, Norbert.' Answered Jack, jovially, his seemingly irrepressible mood buoyant again. He rushed down the stairs, passing me as he went, then chivalrously opened my car door for me when I plipped it unlocked.

I almost smiled and thanked him, then remembered that I wanted to kick him in the nuts again and yanked the car door closed, almost catching his fingers in the process. I couldn't deny that my interest was piqued though. I wanted to see what evidence they had and who the Polish driver was.

I peeled out of the carpark before Jack and Uncle Knobhead got into Jack's car but wasn't concerned about them. They would find their own way to the office.

Filtering into the traffic out of Maidstone, I called Patience. There was a chance she wasn't up since she was still taking time off, but I had a task that would be more fun with her along.

The call connected, and her voice exploded onto the line. 'Yo, skinny white girl. Whatcha doing?'

'Good morning, Patience. I am on my way to work.'

'Still investigating aliens?'

'I am actually. I have two college boys I need to speak with later, I thought you might like to tag along and maybe get some lunch afterward.'

I heard her stifle a yawn. 'What time do you need me?'

'Not for a couple of hours.' I heard another voice in the background. 'Where are you?' Then my senses caught up with me. 'Oh, God, you're with someone. Sorry.'

'I'm at home, dummy.' Sensing my embarrassment, she added, 'Now don't worry about interrupting Patience. I was just giving him a few minutes to catch his breath anyway. I need an hour, so collect me when you are ready.'

She disconnected.

Patience went through men with such regularity that I doubted she even bothered to learn their names half the time. The two of us had very little in common. Our attitudes toward men, life, work, career were all poles apart, but I loved her like the sister I never had.

We hadn't seen each other for a few days. Since I left the police service, we no longer spent time with each other through work and had to find time to do things together. We were going out tomorrow night but there would be a dozen other girls out with us and no opportunity to talk. Lunch by ourselves was appealing.

I hadn't seen Brett last night as we had planned and now, I was out Saturday night so wouldn't see him then either. Could I take him to the girl's night with me? I toyed with the idea for about half a second until I ran through the scenario of him meeting Patience. I doubted our relationship was strong enough for that yet. Maybe after the wedding.

Joking aside, I wanted to see him tonight. I thumbed a button on my steering wheel to activate the phone and spoke his name into the microphone. It autodialled his number.

'Good morning, sexy.' His deep, manly voice instantly sent sparks through me. 'I missed you last night.'

'I missed you too.' I lied. I had just about managed to brush my teeth before I fell into bed. I had been asleep less than five minutes after getting home and hadn't had time to think about him and what we could have been doing. 'I needed to call you about Saturday.'

'Yes.' He murmured. 'I wanted to talk to you about Saturday as well. About how I am going to use one hand to pin you against the wall as I kiss your neck. I'm going to make sure you cannot escape as I rip off your...'

'I am out Saturday!' I interrupted quickly. I could feel my body beginning to react to his whispered dirty talk.

'Oh.' He said, disappointment heavy in his voice. 'I thought you said you were seeing me.'

'Yes, I did. Sorry. When you called last night, all I could think about was getting you into my bed and I forgot that I have a girls' night out in Maidstone. It's been planned for weeks.'

'A girls' night out, huh? That doesn't sound like the kind of event I can tag along to.'

'No, sorry.'

'Well, I can't blame you for having a life. Amanda, I want to say something. It has been bubbling inside me for a while now and I know over the phone isn't the right setting for it, but if I don't get it out, I might burst.'

'Okay.' I replied, suddenly nervous.

'Amanda, I think you are amazing.' He started. This was going well. 'I was so upset when I thought you were seeing someone else, that even when I was in Costa Rica, I couldn't stop thinking about you.'

'Okay.'

'I'm not finished.' He insisted gently. I folded my top lip over my bottom one to stop myself from speaking. 'I want you to know that I am falling for you. I can't control it. I have never had this before, never felt feelings like this before.' My heart was pounding in my chest. 'I wanted you to know that. I doubt we are on the same page. I worried about telling you in case I scared you away, but it's done now.' He lapsed into silence.

How on earth do I reply?

'Me too.' I squeaked. I couldn't explain how I felt at the moment. Lighter than air? Giddy? Something like that.

'Amanda, I want to see you again. We both have busy lives, let's make time for each other. I will be available when you are, even if I have to cancel a flight.'

I briefly considered driving directly to his office in Dartford, so I could shag him on his desk. Allowing my horniness to rule my life, make me late for work and all the deceptiveness that would have to go with it was not a road I would let myself go down though.

'Tonight. How about tonight.'

'Text me a time to pick you up and I will be there.'

'Okay.'

'There's one more thing.' He said. 'Something I want you to consider.'

'Yes?' He was clearly holding back from saying it for some reason.

'You don't need to work. I can take care of you.'

'What?' I wasn't sure I had heard him correctly. It had sounded like he suggested I quit my job and have him pay my bills.

'You don't have to work, Amanda. We never talk about it, but I earned more during this conversation than you earn all year. I'm not bragging. It is just how it is. If you wanted to be done with paying bills and…'

'I'm going to stop you right there, Brett.' I was failing to keep the irritation from my voice.

'I'm sorry.' He shot back instantly. 'I have overstepped.'

Damned right you did.

'Please forget I brought it up.' He bid me good day, promised to be waiting and let me go.

In the quiet of the car, I thought about him. His comment about not having to work was troubling but at least he had withdrawn it rather than push the concept. I was too independent to be a kept woman. Ignoring that though, I was falling for him and it was mutual. I shook my head in a physical act to break my train of thought.

Get a grip, Amanda.

I needed to find out more about him. If this was how we felt already, I needed to have a proper conversation about life and kids and plans. If there was a deal breaker out there, I wanted to find it now, not six months after the honeymoon.

My musings had taken me all the way to work where I parked my car in what I had already come to think of as its usual spot. I opened the back door with a key and closed it behind me. As the door closed, I saw Jack's car swing into the carpark. They could come to the front door.

I silently acknowledged that I was taking my anger over their behaviour further than I needed to. I could have held the door for them. I would consider calming down if they didn't do anything to annoy me in the next half hour.

'Hi, James.' I called out as I went into the office.

'Good morning, Amanda.' His voice came back. 'There are clients to see you.'

I had called out to James as I came into the office but had gone into my office to hang up my coat and put down my handbag so hadn't seen the couple huddled on one sofa. I walked over to them now.

'Good morning.' I offered them my hand as they both stood to meet me. 'Amanda Harper. How may I help you?'

The pair had been holding hands and projected the familiarity that one sees with long-married couples. He looked to be about fifty years old and was balding and had a surprisingly round pot-belly protruding from his ill-fitting suit. Next to him, his wife bore no makeup and had styled her hair in a manner that I assumed was easy to keep. It was short with a square-cut fringe. She wore slacks and a coat and running shoes on her feet and looked barely feminine.

He spoke for both of them, 'Maurice Brown and this is my wife Shelagh.'

James had left his desk and joined us by the sofas. 'Maurice and Shelagh have a zombie cat.' He explained. I glanced at him, but he was carefully avoiding betraying any emotion or opinion in his neutral expression.

'Did you bring it with you?' I asked, looking around the floor for a carrier.

'Oh, goodness no.' Maurice replied shocked. 'No, we can't.'

I said, 'Oh.' And waited for him to expand. He wasn't going to though and his wife was yet to speak so I asked, 'Why is that?'

'Because it's dead.' Mrs. Brown revealed in a dread tone.

'Um.' I said. It was all I could come up with as a reply.

'It died two weeks ago.' James explained, once again providing some background facts they had already given. Tempest always said he didn't get many drop-ins. Usually, people emailed or called, but we only moved to this office three days ago so perhaps our position on the High Street

111

would attract more clients that would see the sign outside and decide to pop inside.

Maurice picked up the narrative once more. 'Mogsy, that's the cat's name, died two weeks ago yesterday, but a week after he died, he started reappearing in our garden again.'

'Are you sure it's the same cat?' I asked the obvious question.

'Absolutely.' Snapped Mrs. Brown. 'Same collar, same eyes but it looks dead now and it hisses at me whenever I try to get near it.'

Listening to Mrs. Brown was creeping me out though her zombie cat sounded like most other cats to me. 'Do you have a picture?' I asked her.

She rummaged in her handbag. Behind her, the office front door opened again as Jack, Uncle Knobhead and Bob came in. 'James could you escort these gentlemen to my office please?'

As he dealt with them, Mrs. Brown continued to rummage. 'Oh, here you are.' She said as she took a small white envelope from her bag. It contained two photographs. The first was of her with a large black cat in her arms. She looked to be a decade younger, but the haircut and dress sense was the same. The cat looked young and healthy with a lustrous coat of jet-black fur.

The second photograph was of a manky, flea-bitten cat sitting at the foot of a garden fence. Its lips were drawn back in a classic cat's hiss and it looked ready to take someone's face off. I got what she was saying about it looking dead. It looked dirty as if it had just been dug up. It had a mangled ear and one eye looked to be milky from cataracts. It looked old.

The stand out feature for me though was that it wasn't even the same colour as Mogsy. It was a mottled grey tabby cat.

I held the two pictures next to one another and showed them to the couple. Trying to keep any bewildered amusement from my voice I questioned again whether they were sure it was the same cat.

'Of course, it's the same cat.' Snapped Mrs. Brown, irritation spiking. 'Why do people keep asking if it is the same cat?'

I had to point out the obvious. 'Because they don't look even slightly similar. One is black, and one is a tabby.'

'Maurice we are leaving.' She announced as she snatched the photographs back from my unresisting hands.

Maurice just looked lost, but he moved soon enough when she shoved him toward the door. 'Oh, err, thank you for your time.' He managed weakly as he was propelled backward.

I could hear his wife berating him for bothering to thank me as the door swung shut. I wondered how often we would have to deal with crazy people walking in off the street. When they emailed, we could respond to politely advise that we would not be taking the case. It was less easy when they were stood in front of you and you had to listen to their story to determine that their case was a waste of time.

Tempest was clear that he didn't want the firm to investigate ridiculous cases. There were enough ones with merit around, that we didn't need to charge people money for the ridiculous ones.

James was making coffee for my guests. 'Do you want one?' He asked, holding up a cup.

'Yes please.' I helped him carry the cups back to my office.

As he set the two he was carrying down, he said, 'I have some information pertaining to the case when you are ready.' I also had more that I needed him to research, not least of which was the cryptic message I got from the hoody last night. James didn't wait around to see what Jack had to show me though.

Bob had placed his camera on my desk and was holding an HDMI cable. 'Alright if I plug it in?' He asked while miming plugging it in.

'Sure.'

I was curious enough to let Jack show me his footage if that was what I was about to see.

'This is the raw footage from Milosz Kyncl. He took it on his iPhone yesterday late afternoon, thankfully before it got dark.'

On the screen was a grass bank, which the person holding the phone was scaling. There was a voice rabbitting away in what I guessed was Polish. The grass bank was only a few feet high and dropped away on the other side, where a wide band of low-level meadow led to a woodland. Right in the middle of the shot was an alien spaceship.

What else could it be? The unseen Polish driver's voice was jabbering faster now, excitement and nerves showing. The phone was not being held steady as he moved about but when he stopped moving the… spaceship, might as well call it that, was very clear.

It was shiny like chrome, about six or seven feet tall at a guess and maybe ten feet long. There was a thick mist around it like you get with dry ice and lights beneath the vessel were illuminating the mist in an eerie way.

Then a figure emerged from behind the vessel, and the driver threw himself back down the bank to escape. The camera tumbled with him as he rolled over and over then came upright as he found his feet and stood. He was babbling in Polish still as he climbed into the cab of his truck, the screen suddenly showed the ceiling of the truck cabin's interior – he had put it down facing up. We heard the engine roar to life then a hand covered the screen and the footage cut off as he stabbed the button to end the video recording.

I had been leaning toward the screen, engrossed in what I was seeing. Standing up straight, I caught Jack's expression – he looked triumphant.

'We have over three million hits on the website since I uploaded some short clips of the footage last night. Bob and I worked on the editing all night ready for when the press asks for it. The phone is going to ring any second.' He claimed, taking out his phone and placing it on my desk.

All four of us looked at it. Nothing happened.

'Any minute.' Jack corrected himself.

Still nothing.

'Dammit.' He swore.

I had to admit that the footage was compelling. The world would want to speak with Milosz Kyncl and I wondered if Jack had considered that he might not be the star of this. Telling myself that it was not a spaceship I was seeing told me what though? If it wasn't a spaceship, it was a...

I couldn't answer that yet, but I was going to.

'So, what are you going to do with this?' I asked Jack.

He flared his eyebrows as he grinned. 'Propel myself to international stardom, babe. The next episode of the show will air tonight to millions of live-streaming viewers. You can still be a part of it, you know.'

Uncle Knobhead spoke up, 'Go on, Amanda. It'll be really cool for us to both be on the show.'

Jack gave him a sideways glance. Jack had no intention of putting my scruffy, dopey Uncle on his show. He was just using him in the belief that it would influence me.

'I don't think so.' I replied.

'That clearly wasn't a no.' Jack replied chirpily.

'It most certainly wasn't.' Added Uncle Knobhead.

'No.' This time I made the answer clear.

Jack heard my answer, glanced at me, grinned again and said, 'I'll take that as a yes.'

Bob was unplugging his camera and they were packing up to leave.

'Where are you going?' I asked suspiciously.

'To prepare, babe. If the press doesn't call today, they will after tonight's show.' His confidence was infectious.

I stepped out of the way to let them pass.

My Uncle stopped as he drew level with me at the door to my office. 'I'm going to go with Jack. Is that okay?'

God, yes.

What I thought and what I said were not the same thing. 'Of course, Uncle. I hope he lets you have a spot on his show.'

As Jack walked away, I thought of a question I wanted to ask him. something that had been troubling me from the start. 'Jack.' He turned to see what I wanted, his ever-hopeful expression probably expecting me to say I had changed my mind and would love to be on his show. 'How is it that you came to be at Brompton Farm on Monday? How did you know about any of it?'

'The Supernatural Times, love. I read about the events there on Monday morning. Bob and I were on the road an hour later.'

It made sense, I suppose. I nodded that I acknowledged his answer and let him go.

When they were out of the office I went over to James. 'What have you got for me?'

'Well, you gave me quite a list of subjects to explore. What I have is something interesting about the farm manager Gordon McIntosh.'

I joined James around his side of the desk so I could see what he was looking at.

'He is on LinkedIn and his status says he is openly looking for investors. Look a little further and he is planning to set up a farm. It doesn't say where, but I could call him posing as a potential investor and see what I can learn.'

I considered that for a moment. He was unhappy where he was and felt... what? Undervalued? No longer in charge? Undermined? It could be all of them or his decision to leave, if that is what it was, could be motivated by pay or the ill-health of a family member or anything really. Whatever it was, it wasn't incriminating. But, if he wanted investors, was he trying to buy Brompton Farm? Was he poisoning the cows to make the milk worthless in a bid to drive the current owners bankrupt? I would not put it beyond him.

'Okay. What else?'

'Well, there is more information about him in the pack I sent you. Background stuff mostly such as job history, marital status. Mr. McIntosh is an Army veteran, like Tempest. He served in the Falklands war as a helicopter pilot.'

I filed that away for later. It didn't seem relevant.

'One other thing I turned up pertains to the deceased.'

'Go on.'

'Tamara and Glen were not married. You referred to them several times as a married couple, but they weren't. Semantics possibly, but Tempest tells me to give him all the information because one never knows what might be important later. Also, Tamara was still working in the pharmaceuticals industry.'

117

'I'm sorry?'

'I didn't know if that was important or not, but again, you said that they were farmers and that it had been Tamara's dream to pursue this lifestyle. Well, she was still working away a lot as she went around the country selling drugs.'

I thought about that for a moment, trying to make sense of the new information or to work out what it meant. 'Can you stick with this? See what else you can turn up about the farmers and their staff?'

James said, 'Sure.' Without looking up from the screen.

'I'll let you know when I find something.' His fingers started dancing on the keyboard. I took a pace to my left since I was standing right next to James and in his personal space.

I called Patience. 'Are you alone now?' I asked.

'Yes, honey. Patience is alone. Are we off to bother young men?'

'Sort of. I'll explain on the way.' I promised to collect her in half an hour and went to collect my coat.

Shoving my belongings back into my handbag, I tried to reassure myself that all I needed to do was keep chipping away at the pieces. There seemed to be so many of them though. So many facets to the case. Crop circles, lights in the sky, alien spacecraft and an alien with a freeze gun and the luminous milk that was the one I really needed to solve if I was to be of help to Kieron and the others. I was off to force information out of the two college kids, but I had no idea if they were even involved and whether the appearance of the crop circles had anything to do with anything else.

I hoped I would find out soon enough.

I called goodbye to James and got into my car. On the way to collect Patience, I ran through the case in my head some more.

The crop circles were the first odd thing to happen way back in September. The crop was all cut and stored now so no one could make the circles even if they wanted to. Then the milk, the lights, and the spacecraft had all happened at more or less the same time. How was each of these elements connected?

If I took the line that nothing alien or extra-terrestrial was occurring, then I needed only to figure out what was causing each of the events. That was the difficult bit for sure, and what about Tamara? Someone had killed her. The police were doing something, I was certain of that. I just didn't know what it was and to my knowledge, other than quiz some of the farm hands, they hadn't actively pursued the case.

I tried focusing on one bit at a time. Jack's spaceship footage: It was compelling, but it had to be fake, right? I had seen Sci-fi movies, the effects utterly convincing. Was the spaceship just a well-made cardboard model? Was it clever CGI? If so, then who made it?

What was it Tempest always asks himself? Who stands to gain?

I wound that question around in my head. There was only one answer though – Jack. His Alien Quest show was a rubbish, third-rate internet show that was going nowhere. Would he fake an alien landing to boost his ratings? Probably, but did he have the resources? The thought that he might be behind it though was troubling. If he was guilty of faking the spaceship and the alien, was he also involved in the poisoned milk and the death of Tamara Mwangi?

I had arrived at Patience's apartment where she lived on the third floor and had seen me arrive. I caught her waving out the window that I should stay in the car. Presently, she waltzed out the front door of her block, her hips swaying as she sung along to a song she had caught in her head.

She said, 'Hey, girl.' As she swung into my car. 'Where are we going again?'

'Greenwich college main campus. We have two gentlemen to interview.'

'Couldn't do it over the phone?'

'They hung up on me and then wouldn't answer the phone.'

'Oh, so they are rude gentlemen.' She said, cracking her knuckles and punching her right fist into her left palm in a gesture suggesting future violence.

'You seem tense.' I observed. 'I expected you to be more relaxed after… you know.'

'After getting a large helping of cock?' Patience was always direct and never minced her words. It made me laugh and squirm at the same time.

'Anyone I know?'

'Remember Nathan from the Chatham armed response team?'

'Him?'

'One of his brothers actually. He has a huge…'

'So, the two chaps we are going to see are called Lee Davenport and Christian Rogers.' I interrupted quickly before I got a full rundown of last night's activities.'

'I was going to say ego.' She finished. 'I had to shut him up by making him eat my…'

'They were reading a degree in art, but I cannot see what that would have to do with crop circles. They might not be involved in this at all.'

'Mum's lasagne.' Patience finished, with a tut and a sigh. 'Honestly, Amanda. You think every time I speak, I am going to say something outrageous.'

'That's because you do.'

'Well, he went away this morning with…' she left the sentence hanging so I could interrupt again.

Instead, I filled in the blank, 'A smile?'

'I was going to say *empty balls*, but okay, a smile.'

The drive to Greenwich college wasn't far. From Maidstone, we had to sweep up Bluebell Hill and down toward Chatham where the land was lower as it met the river. Then up again to reach Gillingham. Greenwich college originated in Greenwich (famous for the meridian) on the banks of the Thames, but land prices and lack of room for expansion drove them to build new facilities a few miles south in the Medway Towns.

The gleaming façade of the main building reached into the sky to dominate the site. Young adults in jeans and ratty trainers were everywhere. There were so many of them visible it seemed impossible that any were attending lectures.

Signs led us to a carpark where we had to weave up and down rows to find a space.

'Are we getting lunch after this?' Patience asked. 'Patience is getting hungry.'

'You're always hungry.'

'I worked up an appetite, girl.' I believed her.

The reception area was dead centre of the large building that dominated the site. Inside, it was triple height and far more plush than I expected. The floors were marble and the staircases on either side of the lobby were glass and chrome. Ahead of us, was a desk with two stern-looking middle-aged ladies. Both wore glasses and red lipstick and had their hair drawn back into buns so tight the effect gave them a facelift.

I checked my watch. It was 1043hrs. 'Good morning.' I said breezily.

'Do you have an appointment?' The one on the right said without bothering to look up.

'I do not.'

'Students must make an appointment before they will be seen.' She snapped before I could add anything else.

'I am not a student.' I replied, keeping my tone even and neutral. She was being rude, but I wasn't going to do the same.

Both ladies looked up finally at my reply. 'What do you want then?' The lady on the left asked,

I eyed them both, but I didn't get a chance to start berating them for their rudeness because Patience shoved me out of the way. 'Listen, bitches.' She started. Both ladies gawped at her with open mouths as if no one had ever challenged them before. Patience had dropped her handbag on the counter and was rooting around in it. She pulled out her police ID to show them. 'My colleague and I are looking for...' she clicked her fingers at me while maintaining eye contact with the two receptionists.

'Lee Davenport and Christian Rogers.' I supplied.

'Tell me where they are now, or I will have to get unpleasant.' It was always fun watching Patience operate.

The lady on the right was trying to resist being intimidated though. 'What business do you have with them?' She demanded.

Patience's eyes bugged out. She turned her ID around, so she could see it then turned it back to the lady. 'What does this look like to you? Does it look like a library card?'

'It could be fake. I bet you could buy that on the internet.'

'Don't like the ID, huh?' Patience said while rooting in her bag again. 'How about this then?' She asked as she hauled out her cuffs and baton.

'Oh, my goodness!' The other lady exclaimed. 'Terry this is probably a drug bust. I keep telling you all the kids here have weed. Tell them what they want to know.'

Rather than scared, the ladies suddenly looked impressed. Terry was tapping her keyboard. 'They are both due to be in the Galileo lecture theatre in Hancock wing at eleven o'clock.'

'Do you have pictures of them?' I asked hopefully.

Some more keys were tapped and she invited us to come around to look at the screen. The two boys were exactly as Kieron had described them: Kind of pasty and skinny and covered in pimples. Their hair was unkempt and both wore glasses that had seen better days and were not sitting straight.

Behind us a printer whirred. Terry reached across to retrieve a map on which she drew a line to take us from where we were to where we needed to go.

The odd exchange was done so we thanked them for their time, took our map and set off.

Once out of earshot, I nudged Patience. 'I thought you were going to hit her with the damned baton. You really shouldn't be carrying that thing.'

'Now what fun would that be? Besides, it allows for immediate problem resolution.' She was right on that count but I worried she would get caught one day.

'Did you plan to call them both bitches?'

'No, but I prefer to not think before speaking. I like being as surprised as everyone else by what comes out of my mouth.'

Finding the Galileo lecture hall was easy as there were signs for it everywhere. Students were just beginning to file in when we got there. We had been hurrying our pace as I didn't want to have to interrupt the lecture or drag them out for a little chat. Doubtless, Patience had no such concerns and would happily have made her gregarious personality the centre of attention.

Thankfully, no such tactics were required as the two boys were slouching along the corridor towards us as we arrived. They looked just like their pictures. They might even be wearing the same clothes. I just prayed they had been washed at some point.

'Lee Davenport?' I asked as I moved to bar his path.

They were in a group of six young men, all very similar in appearance until I looked a little closer and could see that one of them was actually a girl.

'Looks like you've pulled, Lee.' She said with a snigger that might have been aimed at him or at me.

'Who's asking?' Lee asked. He looked me up and down as he tried to work out who I was and why I might want him.

'I need to speak to you and to Christian.' I replied without answering his question.

Christian's eyes widened at the sound of his name. 'It's a drug bust!' He cried as he tried to bolt, spinning in place and diving through the gap between the two chaps stood behind him.

If I had reached for him, I would have opened the way for Lee to escape. Lee twitched, but when I didn't move, he stayed in place rather than try to shove by me. Christian didn't get far though. Patience, an old hand at this, had positioned herself quietly behind the group. As he popped out the back of the group, she stepped into his path to body-check him.

His head was down to push between his friends, so he ran head first into her ample chest and bounced off.

'Hey,' said Patience. 'Watch where you are going.'

I addressed Lee, 'We just want a quick chat about crop circles.' He had been looking at Christian where he lay on the carpet tile, but his face coloured now. His friends were starting to distance themselves.

'I don't want to talk to you.' Said Lee with indignation. 'I don't have to.' He sounded unsure about the last bit though.

I could just set Patience on them and that would get them talking soon enough but I tried the peaceful option first. 'You don't have to talk to us, Lee. Neither of you do but not doing so makes you look guilty. Are you guilty?' I asked.

No answer.

His friends had mumbled various excuses and left them behind. The lecture had started, leaving just the four of us in the corridor. Christian was getting to his feet.

I pressed on. 'I just want to ask you a few questions.'

'About crop circles?' He confirmed. He looked resigned to the task.

Christian had found some gumption though. 'Don't tell her anything.' He instructed Lee, letting me know there was something to tell. He swung his head in Patience's direction. 'What are you? Reporters?' He asked us both.

'The fuzz, honey.' Replied Patience.

He looked her up and down. 'You don't look like the police. You're too fat.' Patience's eyes nearly popped out of her head. I cringed. No one called her fat and got away with it.

'What did you call me?' She screeched as she lunged for him

He danced out of her reach. 'You look more like a hooker.' He said as he nimbly sidestepped another swipe. 'A big, fat hooker.' Then he ran out of luck and tripped over his own feet. He went down to the carpet.

'Oh, God,' Murmured Lee as Patience dived after him. In what seemed like slow-motion, she hung horizontally in the air for a moment before time caught up and she belly slammed him into the floor.

The air left his lungs with an ooohff noise but the impact shook the building and drew the attention of the students in the lecture theatre. Faces started to peer through the window in the closed door.

'Hit me.' Whispered Lee.

'Excuse me?'

'Hit me.' He said again, this time with just a little more volume. 'Annabel Saunders is watching. If you strong arm me out of here under arrest I will look like a proper bad boy.'

'I'm not in the police. Only Patience is.'

'I don't care.' He replied. 'I'll tell you whatever you want to know.' Then, when I didn't react, he twitched like something had struck him and shouted. 'Arrgh.'

How do I get into these ridiculous situations?

'Arrgh.' He yelled again, putting some gusto into his act. 'You'll never make me talk.' Then he whispered, 'Just drag me outside and I'll talk.'

Alright. I give in. I grabbed his arm and folded his wrist into his armpit to lift him onto his toes. It was a painful hold that overstressed every joint in his arm so he wasn't faking his expression anymore. 'Which one is she?' I whispered the question in his ear.

'Brunette, blue eyes.' He replied. Behind me, Patience was pulling the deflated-looking Christian to his feet. He was moaning softly and holding his ribs as she nudged him back along the corridor in the direction we had come from.

I spotted Annabel. 'Toughest case I ever had, catching you, Davenport. Let's go.' I pushed him after Patience but whispered that he should struggle and let him resist for a moment before increasing the pressure on his wrist and shoving him out of his dream girl's sight.

At the end of the corridor, we pushed through double doors and into an atrium. Patience was ahead of me, Christian wobbling along uncertainly ahead of her. I let Lee go.

He flexed his arm to get the feeling back into it. 'Are you okay, Chris?' He asked.

Christian gave a thumbs up as Lee crossed the floor to check on him.

'You have some information for me?' I prompted. Now, after all the daft charades, I would finally get some answers.

Lee looked at me, looked at Patience, saw his opportunity and shouted, 'Leg it!' As he grabbed Christian's arm and started running.

In two seconds, they were across the atrium and going down the stairs three at a time. I ran after them, but I knew I had lost them before I got to the top of the first landing. They were younger, faster and desperate to get away.

I stopped and leaned over the edge of the landing just in time to see them run out the door at the bottom, two flights down.

Nuts.

Patience arrived huffing and puffing next to me. 'Next time I see that little dickhead, I'm gonna kick him in the ding ding.'

I felt the same.

I let Patience pick our lunch destination, so, fifteen minutes later we were sitting in her favourite Southern Fried Chicken place in Chatham. It was on the route from the college back to the office, our houses, and the farms so we had to pass it no matter where we were going.

I ordered a buttermilk chicken platter and a strawberry milkshake. Patience got herself a bucket of chicken designed to feed four people. As I picked up a piece of lean, breaded breast meat to bite, Patience pulled a chicken leg out of her bucket with each hand and started tearing chunks off with her teeth.

In seconds, she had grease on her nose, chin, and cheeks and a satisfied look spreading across her face. 'I needed this.' She said between bites.

I cleared my mouth in case she was about to launch into a summation of this morning's activities. I would have implored her to stop, but she was either too hungry to bother or knew that I didn't want to hear it, as for once she just kept on eating.

As I was finishing the last of my fries and she was just getting up to full eating speed with her bucket, she found time to ask me questions. 'Whatever happened to Brett? Are you two done now? Is there someone new?'

'Not much to tell.' I lied. I was trying to avoid talking about it until I knew what *it* was.

'Come on, Amanda. Talk to me while I am eating. Or would you rather I fill in the silence by telling you all about...'

I held up my hands in mock surrender. 'Okay, okay.' I laughed. She would never replace eating with talking but she was probably genuinely curious.

'And you never even got to ride that fine body.' She observed without taking her eyes off the chicken.

'Well, actually...'

'Oh, my God! When?'

I slouched back into my chair. I might as well entertain her for a few minutes. 'Brett knocked on my door on Wednesday night. I think Big Ben went to see him, straighten out what he thought he saw. Anyway, Brett arrived carrying champagne and flowers and there wasn't much talking after that.'

Her eyes were bugging out at me. 'Was it good? Oh, hold on. Was it terrible?'

'It was fantastic, truth be told.' I sighed wistfully. It really had been. Not just because he had taken me to orgasm so many times, but because I was truly interested in him.

Patience waggled a greasy finger at me. 'There's something you are not telling me.'

I was struggling to stop my face from breaking into a smug grin. 'He made it very clear that he is falling for me.'

A piece of chicken fell out of her open mouth. She didn't notice. 'Did he say the L word?'

'No. No, not yet at least. But it felt like he got close to doing so.'

'After one night in bed with you, the fine-assed, multi-millionaire is in love. What have you got between your legs, Amanda? Do your titties dance or something?'

There was a table of young men next to us that was now paying obvious attention to our conversation. This was entirely because Patience was talking about my titties.

As I grew embarrassed by the attention, Patience swung her gaze to lock eyes with the boys. 'Help you with something?' The chap nearest to her tried to clear his mouth to speak but she was in a sassy mood. 'Don't you be coming up with no clever line to throw at us just because the hot girl sitting next to you has titties that dance.'

'Patience!' I hissed.

The boys were laughing now, sniggering at the thought of my titties probably.

I pulled the conversation back under control. 'Brett asked me if I wanted to quit my job. I think he doesn't like that I might not be available when he wants me.'

'Quit your job?'

I nodded.

'After one night in bed?'

'That would seem to be the case.'

'Why not just propose?'

'I got the impression he thinks my job is unnecessary. He earns so much that my wage can be replaced by the change in his wallet, so why not split my time between the gym and the spa and let him pick up my bills?'

'He would just give you an allowance like pocket money? Sounds fantastic. Where do I sign up?'

I chuckled. I was fairly sure she was joking. 'I'm too independent to be kept. Plus... I like my job.' It was true. I couldn't imagine not bringing in my own money and feeling successful.

'You like him though, don't you?'

I shrugged and nodded.

Patience reached into the bucket of chicken again. It was nearly empty, but she came up with a handful of grease-laden fries to devour. 'Maybe you just need to establish dominance.'

'And how exactly would I do that, oh relationship guru?'

'Marmite blow job.'

I waited for a second for her to expand. When I didn't say anything, she looked up from rummaging in her bucket. It was devoid of food now, nothing left but some seasoning detritus in the bottom. As she started to clean her fingers and face on paper napkins she elaborated on her answer. 'You invite him over, get frisky, tell him you want to play a game and that Marmite is one of your favourite things. Then you put some on him and lick it off.'

'Why?' I asked, mystified.

She rolled her eyes. 'Marmite is a vegetarian paste for putting on toast, right? It is basically yeast, right?' She could see that I still wasn't following. 'You will have put yeast all over his knob, so the next morning he wakes up with a dick like a marrow that is glowing red because he has the world's worst case of thrush. Great for getting revenge on cheating boyfriends or for establishing dominance – mess with the woman and suffer.'

My eyes were wide, and my mouth was hanging open in horror. 'How many times have you tried that?'

'Enough to know how well it works.'

'I don't think that is a tactic I can employ.'

'Up to you, sweetie. What's next?'

The task of eating and giving me relationship advice was done. Patience was ready to move on. What's next was a good question though. We had missed the college geeks and they would recognise us now. There were no grounds for arrest, I had only wanted to talk to them but they had resisted and run away as if guilty of something. Now I was more curious than before and had to assume they were somehow involved in the case. At what level I couldn't tell, but it seemed most likely that they were the ones behind the crop circles.

I explained my thoughts to Patience. 'Do we try to catch them at home tomorrow morning?' She asked.

It was a solid tactic. Young men were famous for not getting up at the weekend. I doubted these two were any different. James would find their addresses, but their accents were local which made me confident I would not have far to go to find them.

'I think I need to go to Richard's farm. There are too many elements that don't add up or make sense. I have some questions for him and his farm hands.'

'Okay.' Patience replied.

'You coming with me? I can drop you off at home again.'

It took forty-three minutes to get from Chatham to Cliffe Woods during which we chatted about boys and the night out planned for tomorrow. Linda, one of the young girls at the station was turning twenty-two and had invited all the ladies for a night out in Maidstone. There was enough of us that it would make quite a crowd, but at almost thirty I was one of the older ones and not that excited about it. Patience was a little younger than me and couldn't wait. She was a party girl though, always up for a few drinks and letting her hair down.

Despite my indifferent thoughts on the matter, I was looking forward to seeing some of the girls I used to work with and acknowledged that it would probably do me good to get out.

'Is this the place?' Patience asked as she pointed out the window to a sign. It read Wendle Farm.

I turned the wheel to take my car up the narrow lane. Ahead of us were farm buildings and on either side, there were fields full of cows.

I had seen the farmhouse yesterday but had not really taken it in. Now I was looking at it and had to acknowledge how pretty it was. It was built of ragstone, at least I think that is the correct term for it and only had brick at the corners and around the windows and doors. The roof was thatched, but whoever had done it had gone to extra trouble to weave patterns into the straw and create ornate gable ends. In front of the house was a well-tended rose garden. The roses themselves were nothing but pruned stems at this time of year but I could see it would be pretty in the summer. Smoke was rising from a chimney in the middle of the roof.

I rapped my knuckles firmly on the door. I wanted to ask Richard some of the same questions I had asked Kieron and Glen to see if his answers differed. Thinking about all of that, I almost missed the kerfuffle going on inside. Patience nudged my arm and pointed a finger.

In the window above us, a curtain twitched, and we could hear voices, one man's, one woman's speaking in panicked hushed voices.

Patience and I looked at each other. We were listening to a couple that had just been disturbed having sex. I had been about to knock again but lowered my hand to wait politely instead. Richard and Michelle were a married couple and entirely within their rights to have sex at random times of the day if they so chose.

We heard clomping feet coming downstairs somewhere inside the house, trying to be quiet but not managing to do so, then the door opened to reveal Richard's wife, Michelle.

Her hair was mushed where, in my opinion, it had very recently been getting shoved into a pillow. 'Can I help you?' She enquired as if mystified by my appearance at her door.

I replied with, 'You hired me to solve your alien milk problem. I have questions.' Then I spotted not Richard but Glen in the room behind her. I slipped by her and into the house. The door opened into the main living area so all I had to do was sidestep her to gain access.

'Hey!' She wailed after me, but I was already in her house and looking at Glen. Glen looked guilty and had a sheen of sweat on his face.

If I was a betting woman, I would say that the owner from the next farm was having sex with the wife of his business partner. What did that mean? His wife had died two days ago but had that driven him to seek solace wherever he could find it?

'Glen, so good to see you. Are you well?' I asked. 'You look a little piqued. Like you have been doing something you ought not to be doing.'

'Quite well, thank you.' He avoided answering the sub-textual question. 'Michelle, this is your house, should we make some tea for your guests?'

Patience had come through the door behind me. Largely ignored as Michelle had turned her gaze to follow me, she now strode into the room with her usual confidence. 'I'll have a tea, thanks a bunch, love.'

'Who are *you*?' Michelle asked, annoyed at the interruption and invasion, or perhaps embarrassed that she had been caught.

'I'm Cagney and she's Lacey because she's the blonde one.' Quipped Patience. 'No, hold on. They were both white chicks.' She made eye contact with me. 'What's the one with the two cops where one is black and other is white?'

I thought for a moment. 'Lethal Weapon?'

'Good call.' Said Glen, joining in.

'Does that make me Danny Glover?' Patience wasn't impressed with the comparison. 'We need to work on that.' She said. 'Never mind. I'm Patience, I'm helping Amanda with the weird shit you have going on here.'

Michelle looked confused as well as annoyed and there was no sign that the suggested tea was going to happen any time soon. I had questions though.

'I came to ask Richard some questions, but since you are here instead, I have some for you as well.' I was looking at Glen. He still looked a bit like a rabbit caught in headlights. Like he wanted to bolt but couldn't get his feet to move. Plus, Patience was blocking the door with her arms folded and she looked immovable.

'Err. Okay.' He stuttered.

'Shall we get the awkward bit over with and ask if your husband knows?' Michelle's face took on a panicked expression.

'This was just an accident.' She blurted.

Glen joined in. 'I was feeling sad about missing Tamara. Michelle was just giving me a comforting hug.' At least they weren't trying to deny it. 'We didn't mean for it to happen. Richard is never here for her, he is away from the farm so much... We were both lonely.' His tone had turned pleading.

'It's not really my business. What I really want to know is what you think is causing the milk to glow?'

'I couldn't possibly say.' He replied after a brief pause. It was the answer I had expected but I wasn't really asking it to get an answer, I was more interested to see how he would answer. Whether it felt like he was telling the truth.

'Do you think it is aliens come to invade us and mess with our tea?' My question sounded sarcastic, but I delivered it with a flat, serious tone.

'Why are you asking us?' Michelle demanded. 'We are paying you to find out, not to question us. If we knew what was causing us to lose all our income, we would have solved it ourselves.' She crossed the room and took a seat at the dining table. She sounded like Lara in her attitude toward me.

'Fair point. However, it is my experience that...' My phone pinged with an incoming text. I ignored it even though I knew it would just ping again in a few seconds. 'the people that hire me know more than they share and only admit so when the truth is finally exposed.'

I let my statement hang in the air for a second. I was accusing them both, but not of anything specific. 'Can we talk about Tamara? How long were you married?' I had speared Glen with my eyes. I knew he hadn't been married, what lie would he tell?

'Tamara and I were never married. After a few years of living together, we just fell into a routine of saying we were. Common law marriage – it's a regular, everyday term.'

Yes, it is. Good answer.

So, Glen was able to respond with an answer that worked. It admitted the truth but didn't expose him.

I nodded and changed tack. 'The milk at each farm was affected a few days apart, first yours, then Richard's and then Kieron's.' I got the order wrong deliberately. 'What do you think of that?' I didn't know what I was asking, this was an old technique though. Glen had been answering my questions so I was continuing to fire new ones at him. At some point, he

137

might say something that would allow me to ask a more pertinent question.

'Mine was the second farm to be affected.' He corrected me.

I nodded, making a mental note. Then turned my attention to Michelle. 'How do you know, Lara?'

She took a seat at the table, cradling her bump as she did. 'We met at university. We were in the same class and discovered that we both came from Exeter. That was enough to get us chatting and we hit it off.'

'What were you doing in Rochester when you met Richard?' The chaps had said they were in a bar when the two girls wandered in, but the girls were not local so must have travelled for a reason.

Michelle seemed stumped by the question though. 'I don't recall. It was a long time ago.'

'It was last year.' I pointed out.

'A lot has happened since. I think it was a concert. Yes, yes that was it. There was a concert at the castle in Rochester and we were there for that. We were early so we went for a drink. That was when we met the chaps and we got talking and missed the event anyway.'

She was lying. I saw people do this all the time during an interview. Once she had a second to dream up a story, she had gone on to embellish it with some details.

I locked eyes with her. 'Who was playing?'

'I'm sorry?'

'At the concert. Who was playing?'

Again, she struggled. 'A local band. Local to us in Devon, that is. I forget their name now but they were touring so we followed them.'

I didn't need to hear who it was. I could expose the lie by quizzing Lara about the same subject. I thought briefly about calling her now but dismissed the notion. It wasn't important. The important bit was that she was lying and I needed to find out why.

I had come here to talk to Richard. He was unavailable but I was learning more from these two than I expected. Catching them having sex… well, I wasn't sure what that told me yet, but it changed my perception of the relationships between the main players in this mystery.

I had more questions to ask, however, I wanted some time to think first.

'Patience, I think we should leave.'

Michelle responded with, 'I think you should too. You are wasting our time with your ridiculous investigation.'

I had been turning toward the door, but her open hostility stopped me. 'Is that what Richard thinks?' I asked.

It was Glen that answered. 'Richard means well. So does Kieron, but I don't see what one *girl* can do in the face of an alien invasion.'

I ignored the barb about my gender. 'You seem like a rational man, Glen. Do you really think the problems here are caused by visitors from another planet?'

'Yes!' He replied with a frustrated tone as if it was already proven. 'They have been seen. There is evidence all around. My wife was killed by one this week.' He slumped into a chair looking defeated. 'I would run away, but where would I go? Where would be safe?'

Michelle crossed the room to comfort him. I indicated that we should leave and followed Patience out the door.

Back outside the farmhouse, I didn't go back to the car as I had intended. Instead, I wandered across to the milking shed. I was beginning to see the difference between the buildings now. Patience trailed along behind me, no longer bothering to ask where I was going.

It was early afternoon on the farm, workers were performing various tasks and the cows were being milked. Even though the milk was unfit for human consumption, they still needed to milk the cows.

I checked over my shoulder; if Glen and Michelle were watching I couldn't see them. I walked into the cowshed.

'It stinks in here.' Patience complained. 'I'll wait by the car.'

I opened my mouth to argue, but she was right, it did stink. I closed my mouth because I was breathing it in. I wrinkled my nostrils. There were several guys ahead of me, I wandered over to them.

'Hey, guys.' They hadn't seen me approaching, as they tended the machinery. I had to speak loudly over the din the cows and the machinery created. 'I'm Amanda Harper, I'm investigating the milk problem. Do you mind if I ask you a few questions?'

'No. Fire away.' The one that answered had a mop of unruly black hair that went well with his easy smile. His colleagues neither spoke nor disagreed with his answer, but all three gave me their attention.

'Do you work on all the farms or just this one?' I posed the question to the group.

Again, it was the mop-haired spokesperson that answered. I wondered if he was a supervisor or something. 'Mostly here, but occasionally one farm in the cooperative has a task that needs more hands. We haven't been operating like this for very long, not yet a year, so we are still working out how to manage the farms in the most economical manner.'

That was my easy opening question to get them talking. Now to see if I could get anything worthwhile from them.

'So, you work for Richard primarily, yes?'

They all nodded.

'Is he away a lot?'

'Away?' the spokesman asked. 'As in not on the farm.' He clarified. 'I don't remember the last time he wasn't here.' He checked with his colleagues, but they all concurred.

'But he is not here now.' I pointed out.

'He is working one of the fields. He is very hands-on, both he and Mr. Fallon are. I think they like to be seen as proper farmers rather than owners.'

'What does working a field entail? How long would he be doing that typically?'

Mop head smiled. 'Well, it takes Richard all day, but it is only a half day job. We don't like to point out how slow he is, given that he is the boss. He is out there with the ploughing gear turning the field.' He saw that I still wasn't following and expanded his answer. 'The crop was cut a few weeks back. It then gets collected and baled using that piece of kit over there.' He pointed to an alien-looking machine parked off to one side outside the milking barn. 'Then, when time presents itself, we turn the field to shift the roots of the wheat. The remaining organic matter will then rot more quickly and be ready for a fresh crop to be planted next season.'

'So, with Richard off to work a field, you can predictably expect him to be gone most of the day.'

'Absolutely.' Mop head replied as the others all nodded their agreement.

Hmmm. 'How often do you see Glen here?' They had lied about Richard being away or had at least been convenient with the truth. They had made it sound like he was off on business for days at a time leaving his wife lonely and in need of company. What else had they lied about?

'Mr. Adongo? Now and then, I suppose. Why do you ask?'

I shook my head. Then changed my mind. 'One last question. When was the milk here first affected?'

'A couple of weeks ago.' Answered broken nose. Now that he had found his voice, he was full of answers. It matched what I had heard from everyone else.

'Why do you think this farm was affected first?'

Broken nose kind of shrugged.

Mop head was wrinkling his brow though. When I looked at him, he said, 'No. it happened at Mr. Adongo's farm first about a month ago.'

'Really?' Broken nose looked unconvinced.

'It was just a handful of the cows. Derek called me over to take a look at it. He was in a panic because he thought he had done something wrong. I figured something had got into the machinery, so we ditched the milk, isolated that set of pipes and thought no more of it.'

'And this was, what? Two weeks before Richard's farm was affected?'

Mop head nodded.

Someone had run an experiment first to see what happened!

I thanked the chaps for their time, left them there and went in search of Patience.

My phone pinged with another text message. It was in the back pocket of my jeans.

Fishing it out I saw instantly that it was from Brett. My heart skipped as I pressed the icon to open the message.

Hey, sexy. Just wanted to make sure we are still on for tonight. I have booked us a table at Brasserie de Mere in West Malling. They serve the best lobster and mussels. I will pick you up at seven. Let me know if you want me to arrive earlier or later xx

I replied.

That sounds wonderful. I am already hungry thinking about the food, and about your body. Would you rather just come to mine and order Chinese takeout afterward? xx

I deliberately didn't say *after what,* as I hoped it would be obvious and would result in his arrival at my flat in a state of excitement, but without the certainty that we were going to get straight down to it.

Before I got to my car, his reply pinged back to my phone.

Your plan is far superior to mine. I'll see you at seven xx

I reached my car and clambered in.

'Wow.' Said Patience. 'Did you just have sex in the milking shed with all those guys?'

'No!' God, what a thought.

'Well, girl, you did something because your eyes are dilated, and you have the red skin thing you get on your neck going on. That only comes out when you are turned on, I know that much about you.'

Panicked, I flipped down the sun visor to check myself in the mirror. She was right. I had never noticed that I did that. I could feel the warmth coming from my cheeks.

'Girl, you better tell me what you been doing now.' Patience demanded. 'I might need to crack a window with the heat coming off your face.' She always loved poking fun at me.

'I was texting with Brett.' I admitted haughtily. He was my boyfriend and I was allowed to exchange saucy messages if I wanted to.

'Show me.' She begged. 'Show me, show me, show me.'

'No.'

She made a grab for my handbag.

Surprised, I shouted, 'Get off!' As I yanked it away, but she managed to snag one handle and had her hand inside it rooting around for my phone.

'Show me your dirty messages, Amanda.' She pleaded as I smacked her hand away and reclaimed my belongings.

A rap on the window made me jump. 'Everything alright, ladies.' Asked mop head through the window. 'I could see what looked like a fight.'

I powered the window down. 'Sorry. My friend and I were just leaving.'

'You dirty girl.' Patience had found my phone while I was distracted and was reading from the screen, the light of it illuminating her face.

I lunged for it. 'Give that back.' She put out a hand to hold me back as she scrolled through the messages. I tried to punch her in the ribs but got her right boob instead.

'Ow! Amanda.'

I snatched the phone back. 'These are private messages, Patience. I don't want you to read them.' I could hear a whining tone in my voice. I turned back to mop head, but he had gone.

'You are too uptight, Amanda. That man of yours is fine so I am glad you have a booty call arranged for tonight, but you could whip him into a frenzy with a few choice words.' I could tell that she was waiting for me to ask her what I should have written. When I didn't, she pressed on anyway. 'If it had been me setting up an evening of...'

'Intimacy?' I filled in the blank.

'I was going to say cock play, but okay, intimacy it is. Then I would have written...'

As I reached the end of the path that led from the farm to the main road, I had to pause to let a procession of vehicles go by. I was looking for the last one to go by so I could pull out when Patience asked, 'What's BARF?'

At the mention of the name, I looked at the vehicles more closely. I had thought they were Army trucks, out here to do some kind of manoeuvres or something. Now I was looking though, I could see that the camouflage painted on the outside was a deep crimson and black.

On the side of each vehicle, was B.A.R.F. in three feet high capital letters. I debated following them, but I had no idea where they might be going or how long I could be tailing them for. On top of that, I wanted to hear what the crime scene guys had to say and needed to go via Rochester High Street first.

The last truck went by, giving me a chance to look into the back of it. There were troops inside. I couldn't get a good look at them, but there were definitely uniformed bodies sitting on the bench seats within. I made a mental note that BARF was, in fact, real, and pulled away.

As I drove back to Rochester, Patience regaled me on the finer points of getting men horny. I'm not going to repeat what Patience would have written in her version of my text to Brett, but it was horrifying enough to make the wax run out of my ears. It was my experience that getting a man horny really didn't take much, but perhaps there was something I could learn.

Coming through Strood, she finally finished and fell quiet. In the silence, I remembered that I needed to check in with the crime lab guys. I called the main line to the lab itself rather than Simon's cell phone.

'Crime lab.' Steven answered.

'Hi, Steven, it's Amanda. I had a text from Simon to say he had news for me on the items I dropped off yesterday.'

'Ah, yes. Did he also say that we are holding the information until the ransom is paid?'

He was on speaker in the car, so Patience heard what he was saying as well. 'What ransom?' She asked.

'Donuts.'

'Is that Patience I hear?' Steven asked.

'It is. We have been investigating. Now we are on our way to Mr. Morello's Royal Cake Shoppe in Rochester to buy your donuts.'

Patience's head and eyes whipped across to stare at me, her excitement visible.

I disconnected the call. 'What?' I asked her, knowing, of course, exactly what she was getting excited about.

'We're going for donuts at Mr. Morello's?' She said his name with reverent respect.

'I promised the chaps at the crime lab I would get them a box for helping me out again.'

'Ohmygod, ohmygod, ohmygod.' She began doing a happy dance in the car. 'Donuts, donuts, donuts.'

I had eaten cakes at Mr. Morello's place before, so I knew that not only was everything inside the hallowed walls fantastic, but the chaps at the crime lab would see that I had gone to some extra effort, rather than get them a tray from a supermarket. It was a mark of appreciation for their help.

Patience reached over to grab my wrist. 'Drive faster.' She instructed, although I could not tell if her tone was mock-serious or if she really meant it.

'What?'

'I mean it, Amanda. I love you like the skinny white sister I never had, but if you don't hurry up, there's going to be trouble. Patience needs a donut.'

I laughed at her and put my foot down.

It was already twilight by the time I parked the car in its spot behind the office. Since James was now working full-time hours, he would still be there. I could have checked in on him by phone but dropping in seemed not only friendlier but gave me the opportunity to have him show me things on his computer.

'Where are we going?' Patience wanted to know.

I unlocked the back door to the office and pushed it open. 'This is the new office. Tempest rented it on Monday and we moved in on Tuesday.'

'What happened to the old place?'

I stopped to turn and look at her. 'It burned down?' Surely, she remembered that happening.

'Oh yeah. Sorry, I'm feeling a little woozy, my *blood sugar* must be getting low.' She raised her voice when she said *blood sugar,* so I would understand I was delaying her rendezvous with the donuts.

'This won't take long.' I assured her with a sigh.

I led her down the short corridor at the back of the office which linked the outside with the inside and kept the storeroom and toilet hidden from view in the main office area. The next door, which opened into the main office, also had a lock but we never bothered with it. Tempest reasoned that if someone had gone to the trouble of breaking down the first door, they would just keep going so we would have two broken doors to fix instead of one.

I pushed it open and called out, 'Hi, James. It's Amanda and Patience.'

It wasn't James inside though but Jane. I hadn't seen my cross-dressing, gender-neutral colleague as a girl for more than a week. She was wearing thigh-length, tan-leather boots over cream leggings and a chunky-knit brown jumper than hung loose off her right shoulder to show the lacey strap of her bra. I hadn't known Jane to wear a bra before – there was nothing to put in it after all, but we had dressed her up as bait for the voodoo priest and convinced her to wear one at that time. Perhaps she had decided she liked it. I wasn't going to ask.

'Hey, you've got tits.' Pointed out Patience.

Jane's face reddened beneath her makeup. I elbowed Patience to shut her up.

'Hey.' She said, rubbing her arm. 'I'm just saying. It completes the picture.' She switched her focus to Jane. 'What size did you go for? They look kinda small.'

'Um.' Said Jane.

'I'm just saying. If you can pick whatever size you want, why pick small?'

I changed the subject. 'How has research gone today?'

Thankful to be able to talk about something other than her fake boobs, Jane swivelled in her chair and got up. 'Not bad. You ladies want some coffee?'

'No.' said Patience. 'We are going for donuts. Aren't we, Amanda?'

'Coffee sounds great.' I replied because it did. 'We have time for a coffee, Patience.'

I could hear her muttering under her breath as Jane and I started fiddling with the new coffee machine. She flopped into one of the chairs, feigning exhaustion from lack of food.

'Tempest has been quiet today.' Jane observed. 'He usually checks in towards the end of the day to see what enquiries have come in or to ask what I have been able to find out if he has asked me to do research. Nothing from him today though.'

'Are you doing research for him?'

'No. He is in the middle of that witch case. It seems to be driving him nuts like he cannot work out how the witch is killing with lightning or even who she is or what is motivating her. He did say that Frank had an explanation for him as usual. Not one he believes, I expect. He is certain there are four wives that are guilty, but he can't prove it.'

Hmm, Frank. Would Frank be able to shed any light on my case? Tempest often went to see the slightly-odd, occult bookshop owner because he had an explanation for everything Tempest came across. The explanations were always bonkers, yet Tempest seemed to use them to find a way to the truth. Maybe I should try the same.

I remembered something, 'Did I hear that his client is in the hospital?'

'Yeah. Anthrax poisoning. Can you believe that? Of course, Tempest blames himself for not solving the case sooner.'

The machine was delivering thick dark liquid and filling the office with the wonderful aroma of roasted coffee beans.

'I dug up some information for you on the clients in your case.'

'Do tell.' I begged.

'Want one?' I offered a coffee to Patience who declined. She was fiddling with her phone and paying us no attention.

'Well, you know that Glen Adongo and his partner weren't married. I also found that Glen wasn't a farmer like you said.'

Now she had my attention. 'What was he?'

'A geologist. He came to the UK ten years ago and got a job at a University teaching the subject.'

He lied. He lied about it all. Had he ever been a farmer? And what about his partner? Was the relationship fake?

All I was doing was generating more questions. 'Anything else?' I asked.

'Not yet. I'll keep on it though.'

I thanked Jane for her help, slugged down the last of my coffee and picked up my bag. Patience was instantly on her feet.

'Time to go?' She asked, her feet almost vibrating with energy.

'Yup.'

Half a second later, Patience had the door open and had stepped back a pace to allow me passage. Outside it was cool and the twilight had shifted to full dark. A few rain spots were falling. I tightened my coat around my neck and turned left.

'Hold on, Amanda. You're going the wrong way. Mr. Morello's is this direction.' Patience was pointing in the opposite direction to the one I was going. I smirked to myself. I was deliberately making her wait because I knew it would annoy her.

'We have to visit Frank first.'

'What!' Patience was genuinely horrified that I was making her wait yet longer.

'It's just around the corner. I have a question to ask him.'

'Who the hell is Frank?' Patience yelled as she hurried after me.

I had first met Frank about two minutes after I met Tempest. It was a chilly morning that had seen me managing access to a murder scene as part of my duties as a police officer. Tempest's arrival had heralded the start of a shift in my life and acted as a catalyst to my transition from uniformed service to independent investigation.

Frank was an odd-looking man in his early forties that ran a bookshop just around the corner from the office. The bookshop specialised in all things paranormal or supernatural and catered to the endless stream of persons wanting horror comics and movie figurines as well as those that were believers in the occult and wished to seek out publications that would reinforce their fantasies.

Frank was a true believer. That much was obvious to me in the first few seconds in his company and I would have dismissed him as a nutter were it not for Tempest's insistence that he was a helpful resource.

I pushed open the door that led up a flight of old wooden stairs to his shop.

'Where are we going, Amanda?' Asked Patience again.

'To see Frank.' I repeated my previous answer.

'Who the hell is Frank?' It was a cyclic conversation that was about to end as the little bell jingled above my head and Frank's engaging smile popped around the corner of a bookcase to see who his latest customer was.

The smile was attached to the rest of his face, which was unremarkable unless one wanted to remark about how unremarkable it was.

'Someone mention my name?' He said as he emerged from behind the bookcase. He had an armful of books that he had been loading onto a shelf. 'Oh, hi, Amanda.' He juggled the books so he could shake my hand.

'This is Patience, a former police colleague.' I said as she came into the shop behind me.

Patience was looking around, taking in the general décor and tone of the shop. 'Do you murder people in here?' She asked as she inspected a glass case filled with foot-high models from the Hellraiser films.

'Not so far.' Answered Frank's assistant without even looking up. I had met Frank's young, Chinese shop assistant a week after I met him. She had been kidnapped by a serial killer that thought he was a vampire. Tempest described her as a nimble little minx and I got the impression she had a thing for him that he was resisting. Maybe he wasn't. I couldn't tell, but the cool air coming off her now made me wonder if she was used to using her looks to make guys dance and knew she would have no such luck with us.

She was leaning lazily on the sales counter, leafing through a graphic novel. Frank was paying her to do nothing much, but that was his business and maybe she was only here to draw in the geeky boys that bought the comics.

Frank put the books on the counter. 'What can I do for you ladies?'

I opened my mouth to speak but Patience got there first. 'Answer all her questions so I can go for donuts.'

Frank flapped his lips a few times trying to decide what to say. He settled for, 'Okay.'

He turned his gaze to meet mine. 'What do you know about aliens fiddling with cow's milk?' I asked. I had no idea what I was supposed to ask him or what I might learn so I went with a broad question.

'You are referring to the farms in Cliffe Woods?'

I cocked my head to one side. 'How do you know about them?'

'Supernatural Times.' Poison replied, again without looking up.

When I didn't respond, Frank leaned over the counter and produced an iPad. A few swipes later I was looking at today's edition of the Supernatural Times.

'I must say I enjoyed your interaction with Jack Hammer.' Poison said. I assumed she was referring to me kicking him in the nuts. It had been live-streamed to however many people were watching at the time but was now being shared via social media. Poison was finally making eye contact so I saw why she hadn't done thus far: She had a black eye.

Patience went into cop mode. She hated women getting hit. 'Is there a story to go with that eye?' Her tone was soft, encouraging.

Poison flicked her hair, 'I was fighting the forces of evil.' Her cryptic answer providing no explanation at all.

As Patience moved to talk with her, I turned my attention back to Frank. 'Frank, what is this?' I was reading some of the headlines.

'The Supernatural Times has been going for years. They went digital about a decade ago.'

'Yes, but what is it?'

'They focus on the truth behind the regular stories you read about elsewhere or see on the TV. When there is a ten car pile up and they say it was fog that caused it, do you really think it was fog?'

'Yes.'

'Isn't it more likely that the first driver lost concentration because a spaceship buzzed his car or he saw someone teleport on the road in front of him?'

'More likely? No.' I was checking Frank's face to see if he was pulling my leg but he was quite serious.

'What about when people go missing? People go missing all the time. Mostly it is alien abduction, but no one believes it because the government agencies employed to monitor alien activity cover it up. You remember Deborah Houser, the Conservative politician that went missing last year?'

'Yes. I suppose she was kidnapped by aliens.'

'Goodness, no. She is an alien. I found out through BARF. That's the...'

'British Alien Response Force.' I completed his sentence.

'Yes!' Said Frank, clearly impressed by my knowledge. 'BARF monitor for aliens infiltrating government positions and get rid of them.'

'So, BARF is a real thing?' I thought back to my conversation with Fred a couple of days ago. I might have seen their vehicles with my own eyes less than an hour ago, but I was still struggling with the concept.

'Couldn't be more real. So, anyway, I read about the cow's milk a couple of weeks ago. Jack Hammer wrote the report himself. He writes a column for them most weeks.'

'Wait. Jack Hammer wrote the report? When. When exactly?' This was important.

Frank looked confused for a second, then held his hand out so I could give him the iPad back. 'Poison when did Jack Hammer first report the alien milk?' He asked over his shoulder while he swiped at the screen. 'Never mind, I found it.'

The date on the article was October 25th. More than two weeks ago. He lied to me about when and how he found out. He was getting more and more embroiled in whatever was going on. What exactly was he guilty of?

'Thanks, Frank.' I read the article, then absent-mindedly handed the iPad back to him, I was lost in thought.

'You're quite welcome.'

A new question occurred to me, 'Frank, what do you think is happening at the farm?'

He rubbed his hands together. 'I thought you'd never ask. Initially, when I read the first article, I assumed it was another attempt to seed the human race with new alien genetic code. The point being to cause undetectable birth abnormalities in infants that will allow the aliens to control the next generation. They have tried this before with several different food substances but always something that is eaten by a vast majority of the planet like eggs or corn. There was a mass attack on eggs in the eighties. BARF was able to deflect it without causing mass panic by having a politician publicly state that eggs had salmonella in them. It was a close call though. This one seems to have been a misfire as the tampering is so easy to see. When the lights were reported though, my opinion changed to that of several leading theorists who believe we are on the cusp of a new era of human-alien cooperation. They are monitoring us as we monitor them. BARF believe an invasion is imminent, but it is more likely that their intentions are benign, peaceful.'

'Given our mineral wealth, it is fair to assume they would want to exchange technology for resources. They could fight us for it, but why do that if it can be obtained without conflict and loss of life on both sides? However, the video footage that Jack Hammer obtained of the alien spacecraft suggests otherwise.'

'How so?' I asked the question even though I was convinced the man was babbling utter rubbish.

'It was an attack craft. Frank said, knowingly. 'No reconnaissance vessel would carry that much weaponry. Added to that, the death at Larson Farm was clearly the work of extra-terrestrial technology. We don't have the ability to make a freeze ray. All our weapons maim and destroy. The being that used it probably comes from an alien society that has greater respect for the dead and developed weapons that would kill, but leave the body whole for burial.'

I nodded my head because I had no idea how to respond to anything Frank said. To me, he seemed completely rational and at the same time utterly mental.

Patience finished up chatting with Poison. She would not shift from her story that she had been out fighting dark creatures or something equally bizarre. I was ready to go and watching the clock because we still needed to get donuts and get across to Maidstone station to catch the crime lab guys before they left.

When Patience realised I was waiting for her, she gave up trying to get the truth from Poison, wished her luck and roughly shoved me out the door.

I waved goodbye to Frank as the door swung shut behind us. Then we were back out in the cool November air a few seconds later.

There was a storm brewing off in the distance. The dark sky was punctuated by flashes of lightning in the distance. The rumbles of thunder were too distant for us to hear as we hurried along the High Street. There was rain in the air, the fine misty stuff that sticks to your clothes and soaks you even though it looks like nothing.

Mr. Morello's Royal Cake Shoppe was at the Chatham end of Rochester High Street where it was sandwiched between a butcher's shop and a pub. It was closing in little more than ten minutes, so we needed to hurry.

Patience, who was never one to move fast when she didn't have to, was all but running to get to our destination for fear they might decide to close early for once. As the storefront came into view, we could see the shop assistants beginning to clear the shelves in the front window.

'Aaaaargh!' Patience abandoned me because I wasn't moving fast enough and ran at the door with both hands out. A startled-looking assistant, who was about to lock the door, backed away in fear as the crazy woman barrelled into the shop.

By the time I strolled in, three seconds later, she was already instructing them to get a box ready for donuts.

'You know these are not for us, right?' I reminded her.

She had been bent over, scrutinising the donut selection but stood up to stare at me, surprise on her face. 'Well, sure. They are for the crime lab guys.' She had a faraway look like she was doing math in her head. 'They won't want them all though, will they?'

'I am taking them donuts. A full box of donuts because they are doing me massive favours for no cost. So, no, we are not going to eat their donuts. We will be delivering a full dozen.'

She scowled at me and turned back to the girl behind the counter. 'We'll take the dozen, thank you. And I will have three for myself.' She glanced over her shoulder to scowl at me again. Just in case I didn't get the message, she poked out her tongue.

With a dozen mixed wonderful balls of calorie-heavy goodness in my hands and a slow-moving black woman dragging along behind me, I made my way back to my car.

Patience had eaten all three donuts by the time we got there.

Patience used her card to bleep us into the station. It was the first time I had been back since my run in with CI Quinn more than a week ago. It seemed much longer than that as if time moved faster now that I was out of the Service. I prayed I wouldn't run into him today.

Even though I was being escorted by Patience and had every right to be there, I felt like I was trespassing. My steps were fast as I hurried to the crime lab where I could shut the door. It was only a short journey from the entrance to the lab and we only saw a couple of people on the way. They didn't comment on my presence, though my paranoia told me they were running directly to Quinn's office to tell him I was back.

Behind me, I heard a rustling noise. I spun my head to make sure that Patience wasn't eating the donuts. She had held them in the car because I was driving and insisted she could be trusted to carry them from the car to the lab.

Patience looked at me with an innocent expression. The lid of the box was closed. 'Did you just take a bite of donut and close the lid again?' I asked as I eyed her suspiciously.

'Of course not. These are for the crime lab chaps.' She lied.

'So, if I open the box, I won't find a biscotti cream filled donut with a bite mark in it?'

'Nope.' She grinned.

I pushed open the door to the crime lab and stepped inside. Both the chaps were busy doing something scientific. Simon had his face to a microscope while Steven was fiddling with a test tube.

'Hi, guys. I have a dozen scrumptious donuts.'

Patience mumbled something behind me that sounded a lot like *eleven*.

They both stopped what they were doing to scamper over to the donut box Patience was holding. They snagged one each and Patience put the box down on a table, steadfastly making a point of not taking one for herself. I would point out later that she had a big blob of donut cream on her chin from the one she had scoffed on her way through the station.

'You always bring us the weirdest stuff, Amanda.' Simon said around a mouthful of donut. 'Not the donuts. I don't mean them. I mean the evidence you found.'

'Yeah, it is a strange collection.' Added Steven.

I didn't argue. 'So, what is it? What did I actually find?'

Simon reached under a bench to retrieve a box. In it were a test tube that looked to have muddy water inside, the odd metal object which now had a piece missing from it and a ream of paper that looked to have graphs and data on.

'Where's the milk?' I asked.

'In the fridge.' Simon replied, his voice making it sound like I had asked a daft question. 'Which bit first?'

'The soil?'

'There is nothing special or interesting about the soil itself. PH level within tolerance for the area, traces of animal and vegetable matter – exactly what one might expect to find. The odd element was indeed paraffin that had been ignited. You described burnt circular marks on the grass? Well, they were made using something that burned paraffin as a fuel. That's about as much as I can tell from the sample you gave us.'

'Although.' Steven interrupted.

Simon stared at him for a moment. 'Oh yes. There was a surprising amount of methane in the soil.'

'Methane? Okay, so what does that mean?'

'Typically, that concentration of methane combined with some of the other minerals found such as hydrogen-sulphide and nitrogen would only be found at a site where there was natural gas.'

Okay. I wasn't sure what that told me. However, I would research both natural gas and paraffin later and was expecting to find neither was a likely fuel for space travel.

Steven reached into the box to retrieve the metal object. 'This is a magnesium chrome alloy. Nothing particularly unusual about it, billions of components are made from it every year. I haven't been able to trace what it came from, but the lightness and rigidity of it makes its use in the aircraft industry common.'

'Aircraft industry.' I repeated. I was making mental notes.

'Or it might find a use in anything that was manufactured to be lightweight. Something that needed to be man-portable for instance.'

Simon left his place next to Steven, crossed to a refrigerator against the wall behind us and took out my bottle of still glowing milk.

'I would not drink that.' Said Patience.

'In actual fact, you could.' Remarked Simon. 'It is quite harmless.' To prove his point, he took a sip. 'It does have a slight metallic taste though.' He joined us back at the table and placed the milk down between everyone.

We all stared at it.

'This one stumped us for a while I don't mind admitting.' Simon picked up one of the computer printouts in the box to read from it. 'The luminosity is provided by a concentrated extract from the bioluminescent pigment produced by a cuttlefish.'

I took that in. 'How did it get in the cows?'

Simon shrugged but provided an answer anyway. 'Probably ingestion. Bioluminescence is used in medicine all the time. The patient takes a pill and the only side effect is odd coloured pee for about a day. It would almost certainly also affect the blood if one were to check it and definitely milk production but that wouldn't be listed as a side-effect because it would never be administered to a pregnant woman.'

Patience wasn't convinced. 'What do doctors do with it once it is in a person?'

'Steven, would you like to field this one?' Simon deferred to his partner.

Steven cleared his throat. 'There is an opportunity to identify diseased tissue both by the spectral signals from activators or, in some cases, by the differences of the natural luminescence responses. For practical reasons, defined by the sensitivity range of standard luminescence detectors, much of the current medicinal work has focused on the short wavelength emissions driven by laser activation. However, I believe the techniques employed are poised to undergo a dramatic expansion in scope with the advent of higher sensitivity photocathodes with high-efficiency responses at long wavelengths. It will soon be possible to utilize a greater range of emission features. In recent examples there has been success with the detection of cancer, identifying tooth cavities and the suggestion that the non-destructive luminescence probes can distinguish between tissue changes at a very early stage of development.' He checked our faces to see if we had been able to keep up.

The only problem with talking to Simon and Steven was that they made me feel dumb.

Patience said. 'Oh. Okay.' As if she had understood any of it.

Regardless of the science behind it, someone was getting hold of medical supplies and doing so in enough quantities to dope a herd of cows. I did a mental high five to myself.

I had solved the case.

Well, sort of. Knowing how it was being done didn't tell me who was doing it and why. I needed to work that bit out still but it felt like a victory anyway, even if just a small one. I was breaking the case down into manageable chunks. There had to be a connection here with Tamara since she worked in the pharmaceutical industry and was now dead. Had she been knowingly supplying the drugs? Or had she been killed because she caught the person that was taking them to use on the cows? Whichever it was, I had just taken a leap forward.

'Anything else?' I asked.

Both men looked at each other. 'I don't think so.' Offered Simon. 'Do you want the evidence?' he asked, holding the box up for me to take.

I didn't, but I doubted they did either so I took it gratefully and thanked them again.

As we headed to the door, Patience made a big show of having forgotten to pick up her phone. She rushed back to where it was sitting on the table conveniently next to the box of donuts and accidentally snagged another treat from the box.

'I skipped lunch.' She explained to the guys as she shoved the donut into her mouth. 'I need the energy.'

Brett Visits. Friday, November 11th 1900hrs

I didn't want Patience eating the donut in my car because I knew she would spill crumbs and sticky pieces, so she stuffed the whole thing into her face in one go. Then she sat in my passenger seat struggling to chew it. I think we were both relieved when she finally swallowed.

I dropped her off at home with a promise to see her at the bar opposite the club at eight o'clock the next night. All the girls were meeting there for cocktails and a catch up first. It would be too noisy to talk properly in the club.

I had come through my door a few minutes after six with a deep need to get a lot done in a short space of time. I had stopped at the metro supermarket around the corner to grab wine. I knew I was only buying cheap stuff compared to what Brett might turn up with but didn't want to fall into the trap of assuming he would provide the wine, especially after his comment about paying my bills for me.

Now home, I had to quickly tidy the place, get a shower and make myself sexy. Patience had all kinds of advice on the subject, but I was going to do things my way and not put on the nurse outfit she had offered to loan me.

I was hungry to the point that if I didn't eat something, we would be disturbed by my belly grumbling. However, I wanted to order take out to be delivered so couldn't spoil my appetite by eating now either. I settled for an apple and a pint of water which I devoured while I put magazines back under my coffee table and polished the coffee rings from my coasters.

I checked my watch again and set the shower to run while I went into my bedroom to get undressed. Patience thinks I am prudish because I don't want to talk openly about sex and about what I like to do. I'm not though. I think I am sexually aggressive once I am comfortable with a man and I know how to misbehave. As I put my clothes into the laundry basket, I opened my underwear drawer to select what I was planning to answer the door in.

I don't spend much on underwear, but I have some tasteful pieces. The question in my head was whether Brett would prefer a negligee with heels or a bra, thong, suspenders combination with stockings and heels. The extra height from the heels would make it fun for doing things standing up as I would be a better height for him.

I left my options on the bed and went for a shower where I used a fresh razor to take care of fine detail and employed an abundant amount of shampoo and conditioner to calm my paranoia over the smell of cow dung. I had been walking around in it for half the day and was convinced the scent had penetrated my hair.

By a minute to seven according to the clock on my oven, I was sipping a glass of cold, white wine and just starting to feel the cool air as I was standing around in my underwear. I had gone with the negligee option as it fell to my upper thighs and meant I could dispense with knickers which I was sure would have been off me in moments anyway. I clomped across the kitchen area tile in my heels which echoed in the quiet. It was too quiet I decided.

A knock at my door startled me even though it was the only thing I was waiting for. Quickly, I grabbed the remote for my speaker, found some relaxing music and went to the door.

'Hey, sexy.' I purred breathlessly as I opened the door.

'Wow.' Said Jack Hammer.

OMFG!

I slammed the door shut, caught my breath and opened it again. 'What the Eff are you doing here?' I asked through a tiny crack, so I could hide myself behind the door.

'I wanted to invite you along to the show tonight. It is going to be mega!' He was bursting with excitement. 'Get dressed, I can wait. Or, you know, you could come as you are. It wouldn't do the ratings any harm.'

I squinted my eyes at his suggestion. 'I have a date tonight.'

'I could have guessed that.'

'Go away, Jack.'

'What about the show.'

'GO AWAY.'

I could hear someone coming up the stairs toward us. The next moment, Brett rounded the corner and his head came into view as he jogged up the last flight to reach my floor.

Jack turned to see who it was, then looked back at me.

'NOW.' I hissed.

'Will you come on the show if I do?'

'If you don't go away, I will remove your nuts and make you eat them.' I was practically vibrating with a need to choke the life out of him.

As Brett approached, Jack held up his hands in supplication. 'You sure know how to negotiate.' I flared my eye at him. 'See you tomorrow?' He asked.

I opened the door and mimed ripping his nuts off, aggravation driving me to expose myself. The annoying man danced back a pace, threw me a final smile and swept down the stairs, dodging Brett as he went.

'Who was that?' Brett asked as he reached the landing.

I took a pace forward to grab his jacket and pull him into my apartment. 'No one of consequence.' My plan to open the door and take his breath away had been ruined, but I could make up for it now.

As I pushed the door closed, I grabbed the bottom of my negligee and pulled it over my head. As my blonde hair settled back on my shoulders, Brett gawped at me. I was wearing a pair of heels and nothing else. My nipples would have been hard against the cold, but all my thoughts were on what he had inside his pants, so they were erect anyway.

Before he could recover his composure, I stepped into his personal space, kissed him deeply as I grabbed his hands and placed them on my hips, then broke the kiss and took him to my bedroom.

Brett was in the bathroom taking a shower while I waited for the takeaway delivery guy to arrive. I was famished and desperate to get something to eat. If he didn't turn up soon, I was going to start delving into my chocolate bar stash. I had burned a good few calories this evening and had been hungry long before Brett showed up.

Sitting on my couch wearing a towelling robe, I was trying to find the channel on my laptop that would show tonight's Alien Quest feature.

I found it at exactly the same point that the knock at my door finally came. I skipped across to the door in my bare feet, snagged the bag of delicious smelling goodness as I handed the delivery guy a handful of notes and closed the door with a brief thank you.

I was trying to do everything at once as I grabbed the laptop to place on the kitchen counter and opened the bag while simultaneously grabbing a plate.

Thirty seconds later I had eaten ten prawn crackers and had a spring roll to my lips as Brett emerged from my bathroom.

'Hungry?' He asked as I shoved the rest of the spring roll in my mouth. I nodded. Some of my appetites had been well tended to. For now. But I had ignored the empty feeling in my belly for too long.

'What are you watching there?' He had wrapped a towel around his waist and took a seat next to me on the couch where I had taken the plate and was watching Jack Hammer. 'Hey, isn't that the guy that was here earlier?'

I cleared my mouth. 'This is Alien Quest. It's a crap show about aliens visiting earth hosted by an idiot called Jack Hammer.'

'Jack Hammer? Is that his real name?'

'Apparently so. My current case...' I stopped and looked at him. 'Do you want to talk about this? About what I do?'

'Sure, I want to know all about you. About what you do and what your hopes for the future are. I guess we have talked plenty on our dates but not about anything significant. I don't know that much about you.'

I forked a piece of crispy chicken satay into my mouth and pressed pause on my laptop while I thought about how to start. 'You know I am a paranormal investigator, right?'

'Yes.'

'Well, I investigate cases that have no natural explanation from the client's perspective. Sometimes they are easy to solve and there is no crime being committed, just a confused person that believes they are being haunted or something. My current case revolves around an alien invasion conspiracy.' Brett eyed me sceptically. 'Crop circles led to aliens and spacecraft being seen, milk at the farms starting to glow and a death by apparent freeze ray earlier this week.'

'You must be kidding.'

'I wish I was. The farmers are going bankrupt because they cannot sell their produce and they are scared as much as anything else. The frozen person was the wife of one of the farmers.

I made a mental note to call Neville and see what he had determined during the autopsy. I should have done that already but had forgotten to.

'So, what's the link with Alien Quest?' He asked.

That's what I am trying to find out. Jack is involved somehow. I think he might have faked the alien sighting and the spacecraft footage we are about to see. He might be to blame for all of it, but I don't see him as a murderer. Not that one can tell from appearances.'

I fell silent.

'Shall we watch?' Brett asked.

I forked up some more of the delicious satay and rice as I clicked the play button once more.

Jack was on a stage with a large screen as a backdrop. I didn't know where they were filming but it looked very professional for once. He was explaining to the audience that what they were about to see was the full, uncut clip captured by Milosz Kyncl just a little more than twenty-four hours ago. While he was speaking, there was dramatic music playing quietly in the background. It was slowly building in volume until it shut off suddenly when he stepped out of the way and the video footage started playing on the big screen.

Brett was quiet while it played. I had seen it before, so this time I was watching more closely, trying to find the thing that was wrong: A wristwatch on the alien, a fuzziness around the outside of the craft where it had been superimposed by a computer over the background. There was nothing though. It was still as convincing as it had been the first time I watched it.

It ended, and Jack launched into more talk about what the viewers had just witnessed and what this meant for mankind.

'What do you think?' I asked Brett.

'I think two things.' He said, sounding serious for a moment. 'Firstly, the footage looked very real, so whoever faked it has gone to a lot of effort and therefore has something to gain. Secondly, the Chinese food is gone, and my batteries are recharged so I think it is time you had some dessert.'

When I didn't react, he whipped his towel off and stood up. Hanging in front of my face was, well, let's just say it was dessert.

I awoke in bed next to Brett for the second time that week. It was something I could get used to. I was almost giddy with happiness and trying to keep my feet on the ground. When he woke up, we needed to have the conversation about where this relationship was heading. It had almost happened last night when he said he wanted to know all about me, but we had been sidetracked by Jack's show and then by round five. Or was it round six?

I got up to go to the bathroom and found Brett awake when I returned.

'Hey, babe.' He said as I smiled at his beautiful face. 'Did I snore last night? I don't remember falling asleep. You kind of wore me out.'

I slid into bed and kissed him. Just a peck, not the deep, slow version I wanted because it would be an instant prelude to more rolling around on my bedsheets.

I wanted that but wanted to talk first. 'Last night we started having a proper chat but didn't get very far. Can we pick that up?' I asked. I had come to rest partly on top of him. He was laying on his back, so I had sprawled diagonally across the bed with my chest across his tummy and my face against his chest. He was having to look down his nose at me a little bit but if he felt inclined to move, he made no attempt to do so.

'What do you want to talk about?'

I met his eyes. 'Big stuff, I guess. The future. What you want. What I want. Things that might make us incompatible.'

He sat up a little more now, so he could get a better look at me. 'Like what?' He wanted to know.

'Well, like my role in your life and my job. Your comment about me not working was pretty scary.'

'How so.' He sat himself up a little more, so he could look at my eyes.

'I'm independent, Brett. I have lived by myself since I was twenty-two. I earn my own money, I pay my own bills.' I could hear Beyoncé in my head. 'I don't think there will ever be a time when I will not want to have my own income.'

He sighed. 'You're right, Amanda. It was wrong of me to suggest it. I got carried away with the big picture and convinced myself you might want to stop chasing bad guys. I like that you are independent. I will never bring it up again. Is there anything else you want to know? Fire away.'

I played with his chest hair. 'Do you want kids?' This was the big one for me. I wouldn't say I was desperate for kids, I still felt that I was young enough to not worry about my biological clock, but I knew that I wanted children. I wanted them more than anything else in life.

I looked back up at him, waiting for his answer. 'God, no.' he replied, breaking my heart. 'Nasty, annoying little things that poop everywhere and then learn to talk. Do you?'

A single tear rolled down my right cheek. I didn't brush it away and he saw it. 'That was the wrong answer, wasn't it?' He asked quietly. He could see my face.

I shook my head, struggling to find words. The perfect man beneath me was everything I wanted him to be but didn't want the one thing I wanted more than anything else in life.

We were completely incompatible.

Instead of speaking, I lay my face against his chest and closed my eyes. I wasn't going to cry about it. I was telling myself I should be glad that I had found out now and not later. That had been the point of asking the question.

I levered myself off him. 'I need coffee.' I kissed him once on the lips and left the room.

When he found me a few minutes later, I had composed myself and had a mug of hot coffee waiting for him. 'I made you one, but I wasn't sure how you take it.' I sipped at mine as I offered him sweetener, sugar, and milk.

He asked, 'Can we talk?' He looked miserable, but I think he understood that we had reached a wall we could not get over.

'Of course, Brett. I want kids though, and it's too late now to tell me that you do.'

'I might come around to the idea.' He suggested.

'I can't take that risk, Brett. What if you don't? We get married, I wait a couple of years for you to decide it's what you want and then you decide that you don't. Where would that leave me?'

'But I think I love you, Amanda.'

I hung my head and bit my lip. I wanted to say that I loved him too, even after only a couple of weeks of dating. I wouldn't though. I stayed silent instead.

An hour later, I was in my apartment alone. Brett had left forty minutes ago after I told him I didn't think I could see him again. As the door closed, I had started crying, no longer able to keep the wall up that had been holding the tears inside. Now the blotchiness was finally receding from my eyes and I was forcing myself to get on with my day. I still had a case to solve.

I sat down to have a look at the information Jane had sent me yesterday. She had been chipping away at this case with me for the last few days, constantly gathering new details as I asked for them. I thought she was worth her weight in gold, an opinion that was quickly proven when I read through the latest pack from her. The first interesting item I came across was information pertaining to Glen Adongo. I had always doubted his story about being a farmer in Kenya. Maybe the part about his father's farm was true. It didn't matter. The fact was that he had lied about his background. He lied about his past as well. He said he was a farmer back home in Kenya and continued farming when he moved here, but Jane found that he was educated at the University of Nairobi where he received a first in geology. He then went on to teach in Kenya before he moved to London ten years ago.

Jane had been as thorough as she could be, which in her case meant including a full list of all the staff employed across the three farms and basic information about each of them. For some, this was nothing more than birth date, criminal history, and prior employment. She had indicated if she thought any of the people were interesting.

Then I reached the bit about Jack Hammer. As I read the research Jane had performed, the details she had been able to find as she delved into what he was doing, I couldn't help but let a smile creep onto my face. It was time to confront him. I called the number he had given me.

'Jack this is Amanda.' I said when he picked up.

'Ah, good morning, Amanda. I was expecting your call. The position is of course still open.'

'What position?'

'Co-host on my show, of course. that is why you are calling, isn't it? It should be. The phone has barely stopped ringing all night. I am on a BBC 1 talk show tomorrow evening. If you say yes now, I might be able to get you on the show with me. Massive publicity, massive. Watch the sponsors roll in now.'

All I said was, 'Meet me at the office in Rochester in thirty minutes.' I never gave him a chance to argue. He had been pursuing me so doggedly this week that I was certain he would drop everything. On top of the information Jane had provided, I had spotted something myself. Something I was going to make Jack look at and try to deny.

I had dressed already, but I was unhappy with my outfit choice. Today's tasks demanded something that suggested I shouldn't be messed with. Off came the comfortable boyfriend style jeans, t-shirt and Jack Wills hoody I had been slouching around the house in, and on went sheer, black tights, my red and black checked form-fitting dress with the mini-skirt and cuffed sleeves and a pair of black Caterpillar boots that looked like they could kick through doors. I pulled my hair up into a ponytail as if I were going running, added a swipe of mascara and a three-quarter length black leather jacket. My reflection screamed killer-bitch and the boots would be handy if there were anyone that needed to be kicked today.

A little voice from inside told me I was compensating for the loss of yet another promising boyfriend and trying to look tough when I wasn't. It got kicked in the whatnots and told to shut up. I was going to win.

Somehow, I was going to win. Winners make it happen, right?

Saturday morning in Rochester High Street is much the same as any other morning. As a tourist destination, it attracts people from all over the world, but its proximity to Dover meant that most of them were European. On any given day, a walk through the historic streets of Rochester will yield a plethora of accents and dialects. I was a big fan of the place myself, it was so pretty with its centuries old buildings and quaint cobbled streets. The pokey alleyways that hid wonderful shops selling baked goods or artwork were all marvels to explore. Somehow, when winter came, it was even more romantic and when it snowed it looked like a fairy-tale setting.

There was no snow today, but I had been too miserable to eat breakfast when Brett left and then too determined to get out of the house to remember that I hadn't eaten. Now it was nearing lunchtime and I was hungry yet again.

The car had been left in its usual spot behind the office, but where I would then normally open the back door and go inside, I went around the building to the High Street in search of sustenance.

In a few weeks, the Christmas markets would be here every day, giving Rochester a new feel and smell as the scent of Bratwurst and onions or warm glühwein filled the air.

For now, I would settle for a warm sandwich from the coffee shop. The bell tinkled as I pushed my way into the warm interior and joined the short queue at the counter. I checked my watch to see that I still had ten minutes before Jack's half hour was up. I didn't know where he had been when I spoke to him, but if he was too far away to arrive in thirty minutes, he hadn't messaged to say so.

The queue moved forward, giving me a view of the sandwiches neatly wrapped inside the glass stand beneath the counter. I checked to make sure the brie and bacon panini I wanted was there and snagged it as the person in front of me took another step forward.

Serving at the counter was Hayley. I knew her name because it was written in big swirling letters on a badge pinned to her chest. I was fairly certain Tempest had enjoyed a fling with her a while back. They gave off a distinct vibe whenever they got near each other. Thinking about that though reminded me that Tempest never seemed to have any luck with his relationships either. He was seeing someone now, at least I thought he was, but if that was the case, he didn't talk about her and showed no signs of having had an amazing night the night before. I wondered about Tempest sometimes. He was good looking and successful and above all he was nice. He was just a really nice guy. I started to wonder what he thought about having kids when Hayley called "Next, please" and it was my turn to be served. It broke my train of thought and I squashed the idea when it resurfaced again after my order was placed.

I had just broken up with Brett, I didn't need to start something new anytime soon and certainly not with my employer.

Five minutes later, I was inside the office and wishing I had come in earlier to switch the heating on before going for food. The timer was sensibly set to off for the weekends when typically, none of us came in. We could work from home if we were involved in a case. However, I wanted to confront Jack here rather than at my apartment since every time he went there, I was either naked or very nearly naked.

As I chomped through my sandwich, the warm cheese threatening to spill out, I powered up my computer.

A knock at the front door drew my attention. Expecting the person outside to be Jack Hammer and not a hopeful customer with a new problem, I stuffed the last bite of sandwich in my mouth and wiped my lips with the napkin.

'Good morning, Jack.' He was stood outside with his usual jovial expression as if nothing in the world could possibly dent his happy mood.

I was going to give it my best shot.

'I know about the Polish driver.' I said as he came inside.

I watched his face to see how it reacted, but his smile seemed to be painted on. It didn't crack at all. He said, 'Whatever do you mean, Amanda?'

'The driver doesn't exist. There is no such person as Milosz Kyncl. Who was the driver Jack? Was it Bob?'

'What do you mean the driver doesn't exist? I spoke with him myself.' Then his expression finally changed as his eyes widened in disbelief. 'Oh, my God. They got him already. Twenty-four hours and they already made him vanish and erased his identity. Oh, that poor man.'

'What are you talking about, Jack?'

'You think he doesn't exist because he doesn't. He did, but they will have kidnapped and murdered him and then destroyed all trace of him having ever existed. I bet if you went to his house you would find a new fake family living there now that would claim they had been there for years.'

Once again, Jack had an answer that defied logic but also made sense and he was sticking with it.

I wanted to ask who he meant when he said *they* but asking the question would just elicit another tirade of utter nonsense.

Instead, I asked, 'Just how deep in are you, Jack?'

'You have me all wrong, Amanda?' I could hear the fake innocence dripping from his voice.

'Jack it was you inside the alien suit. You are the one that was spotted outside Brompton Farm by Lara Fallon. I think you also faked the spaceship in the footage you are using to make yourself famous.' The tactic of accusing him was a hopeful one at best. I believed what I was saying but I had not one scrap of proof. If he sounded scared and defensive now, I would know I had got close to the mark.

He laughed though. 'Amanda, that is the most wonderful fantasy. How could I possibly have faked a spaceship?'

179

'I'm going to catch you, Jack. I just hope you are not involved in the murder of Tamara Mwangi.

'Good luck with that, Amanda.' He made it sound genuine.

I turned and started walking across the room to my office. 'Come with me, please.'

In my office, the computer was showing the video of his alien spaceship footage. I had pressed pause at a frame that showed the driver's hand. It was only in the shot for a moment and I hadn't seen it at all to start with. The evidence was one of those things that gets lodged in my brain and doesn't reveal itself until later. I had only caught on when I read the report from Jane this morning.

I pointed to the screen. 'What do you see, Jack?'

He leaned in to scrutinise the screen. 'It appears to be a still from the footage poor Milosz Kyncl took. That poor, poor man.' He was sticking with his story and making a great show of his sorrow for Milosz.

I drew Jack's eyes to a point on the screen. On the index finger of the left hand that was caught in the shot, was a ring. Not just any ring though. 'Jack that ring is a Southampton University Alumni ring. I recognise it because my father wore one. I still have it at home. They are not exactly common, but Bob wears one as well. That is Bob's hand in the footage. Isn't it?'

'Do you think Bob can speak Polish?' He laughed.

'No.' I looked squarely at him now. 'I think you got a Polish actor to do a voice over.'

There it was!

His smile had faltered for just the barest moment. A tinge of doubt had crept into his eyes. He recovered instantly though.

'Amanda, if all you have is a ring on a hand, I must beg you to admit that it is circumstantial at best. This is just coincidence.'

'I'm going to catch you, Jack.'

'And I am going to prove you wrong, my lovely Amanda. I'll tell you what. If you can prove that I am a charlatan, with props and clever tricks, I will go on my show or on National TV or whatever you can arrange, and I will admit publicly that I faked the whole thing. However, when I prove that I am not the man inside the alien suit or somehow faking a spaceship flying over England, you will agree to come on my show as co-host for ten episodes. We will be so big by the end of that run that you will not be able to walk away.'

He put his hand out for me to shake. I stared at it, looked back up at him and grabbed it tight. I squeezed his hand while imagining it was his neck.

'Deal.' I said through gritted teeth.

'Super.' He replied. It felt like he was all but laughing in my face.

Jack was gone, and the office was empty once more. I hugged myself against the cool air. It was just starting to warm up, but it was time for me to go.

As I picked up my handbag, my phone starting ringing. It was somewhere in the bottom of my bag and doing a very good job of evading my fingers as they scrambled for it.

If I didn't find it soon, it would go to voicemail. Annoyed, I upended the bag onto the desk and fished the elusive device from the debris. As I stabbed the answer button, I spotted a loose jelly baby that must have escaped its packet a week ago and had been living in hiding ever since. I popped it into my mouth as I took the call.

'Hello, Kieron. Has there been a development?'

'Sort of.' He answered with a voice that held a tone bordering on panic. 'Lara is in labour.' To accentuate his claim, Lara screamed her discomfort. 'We are on our way to the hospital. I wanted to let you know in case you tried to get hold of me.'

'Turn off the damned phone and drive, you idiot.' Lara shouted between breaths.

'Gotta go.' He said, and the line went dead.

Their baby was coming. I felt happy for Kieron and hoped that getting the pregnancy bit over with and having a tiny baby to love would improve Lara's mood. I also felt an enhanced need to solve this case.

Talking to Kieron about developments had reminded me that the case was not only about glowing milk; there had been a murder. Or, at least, there had been an unexplained death and I had planned to call Neville Hinkley and ask him what his autopsy had shown.

I had the phone trapped between my shoulder and ear as I locked up the front door of the office. I needed a few groceries, which I could get from the shop two doors along instead of stopping on the way home.

As I got to the shop, the call connected.

'Neville Hinkley.' I liked that he didn't feel the need to add the prefix Doctor every time he spoke.

'Hi, Neville. It's Amanda. I hoped you could tell me about Tamara Mwangi. What your autopsy found.'

'Hello, Amanda. Still pursuing your little green men?'

'Yeah.' I drawled, showing my exasperation with the case. 'The truth behind the mystery is still proving elusive. Do you think Tamara Mwangi was murdered?'

'To put it simply, yes. The cells of the body react differently when slowly frozen compared to flash frozen, so I was able to quickly dismiss the notion of Mrs. Mwangi being shot by an alien with a freeze ray. There was some post-mortem bruising though, the type associated with moving a body after death. Poor Mrs. Mwangi was stuffed into a freezer somewhere and brought out for people to find her.'

'Was freezing the cause of death?'

'No, she was strangled. I believe they already questioned the husband over it, but he couldn't have lifted the body by himself and doesn't have a freezer that Mrs. Mwangi's body could fit in.'

I knew from my time in the police that it was almost always the spouse. Murders, apart from the ones perpetrated by drunk idiots with guns or knives at night, occurred due to money or passion or more accurately, being denied either one.

Glen had been genuinely upset when I first saw him, but hours later had done a marvellous job of pulling himself together. If he was the killer, who was the accomplice that helped him move the body and where was the freezer? Or, if it wasn't him, who was it? It had to be someone at the farm.

Then, someone walking toward me in the High Street caught my eye. I moved to the side and stopped moving to reduce the chance that he would notice me.

'Neville, I have to go. Thank you for your help.'

'No problem, Amanda. Good luck with the case.'

I slipped the phone back into my pocket and watched. Gordon McIntosh was coming my way and he was wearing a suit. He went by me and into a bank on the other side of the street. Jane hadn't been able to turn up much on him, nothing that could be considered incriminating anyway, but he was no fan of his boss or any of the farm owners. Would he stoop to bankrupting them though? Did he have a plan?

I followed him into the bank where I saw that he was already being greeted by another man in a suit. This one was younger and had a badge on his lapel that identified him as a bank employee. He led Gordon into a glass-panelled office. As the door closed, I could see that written on it was Shaun French, Business Advisor.

I checked my watch. I didn't need to be anywhere until tonight when I was going out with the girls and all I had pencilled in for this afternoon was laundry and household stuff like do my grocery shopping, which I had been meaning to do for days but had never quite found time for.

I sat down to wait. When an efficient bank employee came to check if they could help me, I said I was waiting for a friend. It satisfied their curiosity and resulted in a free cup of coffee which I sipped while I fiddled with my phone and waited.

I watched Gordon through the glass of the small office but nothing in his movements suggested master villain and murderer.

Just as I was getting bored, the two men stood up, shook hands and Gordon was leaving. He strode out the bank door and turned left to go back the way he had come. I debated asking Shaun the business advisor what Gordon had been up to and whether he would tell me if I pretended to be Gordon's concerned niece while batting my eyes at him. I doubted it would work, certain that bank workers are not supposed to discuss customer details no matter what. Instead, I was going to see where he was going.

Gordon never once looked back to where he had been. I doubt many people do, but it meant that following him was easy. My efforts were not rewarded with a big clue though. Along the High Street, he turned down the steps into the carpark opposite the casino and climbed into an old Land Rover Defender. It was the car of a professional farmer but looked out of place against his suit.

He was most likely going home. As the car came level with me on its way out of the carpark, I noticed a sticker on the back-right quarter. It had a picture on it, but it was the words on it that told me what I needed to know. I had my clue after all.

Laundry be damned, I had research to do. At home, I would get distracted by other tasks. Suddenly excited, I turned around and rushed back to the office. Saturday afternoon was going to be when I started stitching bits of this stupid case together.

Sitting at my desk, alone at the office while the world outside enjoyed its day off, it still took ages to find what I wanted. I could have called Jane, she would have found the information in seconds, but it was her day off too.

Finding information relating to the sticker on Gordon's Land Rover didn't solve the crime. It just filled in one small piece of a confusing mess. I needed to speak with him to confirm what I now believed though.

Another part of the puzzle was the crop circles. I reopened the pack of information Jane had sent me earlier in the week. There wasn't much in there about Lee and Christian, but I remembered that they had a Saturday job, both together at a big, out of town entertainment equipment retailer.

It was Saturday, so I could expect to catch them there.

Just then, I heard a letter drop onto the carpet tile under the letterbox at the front of the office. I glanced up automatically. Above the frosting that went from the floor to a height of about five feet, was my mystery hooded figure, peering through the glass at me.

He had just put something through the door and was now waving his arms at me, gesticulating that I should get on with it or that he was getting impatient with me. I was getting fed up with the cryptic clues that weren't helping me at all.

I ran for the front door, but I had locked it when I came back to stop people wandering in from the street outside. By the time I got it open, he was long gone.

I turned the new envelope over in my hands. It was unmarked, but that didn't mean that the person hadn't left a fingerprint on it. Or on the letter inside. I took it back to my desk, holding it carefully by one corner. It is notoriously difficult to get fingerprints off paper. They are there if the person has touched it with bare skin but almost impossible to make visible. It took clever equipment that had been specifically designed for the task. The type of equipment the chaps at the crime lab had.

I wanted to read whatever cryptic note was inside though, which I achieved with the use of some contact gloves and a pair of tweezers to keep my own fingerprints from entering the equation.

The note bore a new cryptic clue:

It's all about fracking!!!

The triple exclamation point reinforced the frustrated gesticulation I saw through the window. Mystery hoody thought I was being thick and had missed the point.

The task of intercepting Lee and Christian at their Saturday job moved down the priority list as I settled into my chair once more and typed *fracking* into a search engine. I wondered how long this would take.

Finally, I was home after what felt like a long, yet unproductive day, I set my bath taps to run, dropped in a bath bomb and went in search of food. As steam billowed out from my bathroom, I diced some veggies and threw them into my wok. I would have a Spanish omelette thing on a plate in ten minutes and be slipping into hot, soapy water in fifteen.

While I stirred the onions, peppers, zucchini, and mushrooms, I tried to focus on the case. I now had some parts of the puzzle clearly laid out in my head. Jack was the man in the alien spacesuit, I was certain of that. He had lied about everything so far and needed the publicity to save his rubbish show from obscurity. He wasn't the one doping the cows though. That task fell to someone else, but they couldn't achieve it alone, so although I suspected someone, I couldn't work out who their accomplice was or why they might be helping unless it was money.

The fracking clue had turned the case on its head but in a helpful way. My mystery hoody might have been getting frustrated with my lack of progress, but I was never going to work it out by myself.

As I chased the veggies around the wok, I considered what I knew. I knew that it wasn't aliens putting bioluminescent medicine into the cows. This was a big piece of the puzzle, but so far, the one person that had access to medical supplies, Tamara Mwangi, was dead. Her career in the pharmaceutical industry would have given her the opportunity to obtain the bioluminescent drugs that were getting into the milk. I was sure I knew what was causing the lights in the sky and needed only to ask a few questions to prove it, but my efforts to question Lee and Christian had still not yielded a result. The crop circles were proving to be less and less likely to be connected to the milk and the murder and the alien. I was still pursuing them because I wanted to close the case completely and have all the questions answered. It was what Tempest would do.

I kept going with my mental checklist as I served the omelette to a plate and sat down to eat it. I remembered BARF. They were real. It sounded ridiculous, but I had heard their name from more than one person now and had witnessed vehicles with the name emblazoned on the side as they sped by me.

Alien. Crop Circles. Light in the sky. Glowing Milk. A murder. BARF.

By the time I had soaked in the bath for forty minutes, cooled down and dried off, I had still not developed a working theory for how the elements were connected. I put some music on, banished the case from my thoughts and got dressed ready to go out.

Despite what Patience thought of my outfit choice, I went with the satin blue halter neck top from Hobbs and my best pair of skinny blue jeans. I plugged in my hair straighteners and pulled out the stool I used to sit at my dressing table. I had a folding three-sided mirror for putting on makeup and checking my complexion. I looked at my skin now, critically examining it to see if I was aging. Someday a wrinkle would appear at the corner of my eyes. I didn't want that day to come, but the horror of it made me check myself to make sure it hadn't happened.

As my hair straighteners beeped to let me know they were ready, there was a knock at my door. I wasn't expecting anyone and the last person I found outside my door was Brett.

I wasn't wearing any makeup so whoever was out there was going to have to put up with haggard, tired-looking Amanda. The person outside rapped hard on the door again.

'Okay, okay.' I muttered as I crossed the room.

I peered through the spy hole to find Patience outside. She had on a party dress that was two sizes too small for her enormous boobs and had probably been bought for exactly that reason.

'What are you doing here?' I asked as I opened the door. Then I saw that she wasn't alone. I had never met her sisters but if the two women with her were not related to her then I was going to be shocked.

'Have you ever met my sisters?' Patience asked as she barged in uninvited, a bottle of sparkling wine in one hand and a bottle of apple sours in the other.

188

'Hi, I'm Charity.' Said Charity, as she followed Patience into my apartment. She was the same height and the same shape as Patience but a couple of years older and had children where Patience did not. Her hair was braided into long strands that might have fallen to her waist but were wound around and onto her head where they were pinned in place with dozens of sparkly pins. She had on killer heels that made her at least six feet tall and a sequinned black dress beneath a faux fur, full-length winter coat. She looked ready to party hard.

I knew Charity was Patience's older sister which made the third woman her younger sister, Hope.

'I'm Hope.' Her younger sister said helpfully. Unlike her sisters, she didn't invite herself in but put out her hand for me to shake. 'Thanks for looking after Patience. She talks about you all the time, about how you keep her out of trouble and all.'

I wasn't sure I did any of that, but it was nice to hear, nevertheless. Hope was dressed much the same as her two older sisters, but her figure was more athletic and her bust less gigantic, and she was tall. She had on heels as well, but she had to be six feet tall in flats.

I invited her in and turned to find Charity sitting on my couch getting comfortable and Patience wrestling with the cork of the sparkling wine. It popped out and banged on the ceiling before coming to rest by my toaster.

'Wine or apple sours?' Patience asked, holding both bottles, a wide grin plastered all over her face.

'I thought we were meeting at Bar Nineteen?' That was what we had arranged. Bar Nineteen at eight o'clock. I remembered the conversation quite distinctly.

'Uh huh.' Said Patience. 'I knew if I didn't come over to help you get dressed, you would pick out some dowdy old outfit and scare away all the men.'

Dowdy?

189

'I look okay, don't I?' I asked the room.

'You look lovely, honey.' Said Charity from her seat on the sofa. She gave me an encouraging smile like I was six and had learned to spell something difficult. 'But,' she drew the word out, 'It's more of a going to the launderette outfit than it is a going to the club to make men stare at you outfit.'

'Damn right.' Agreed Patience. 'So, we are here to help you slip into something less comfortable and more... exciting.'

'I don't want men to stare at me.' I really didn't. I got enough of it no matter what I wore.

Charity disagreed. 'Of course, you do, honey. Men will stare and then they will buy us drinks and the club security will let us in for free. It's how we roll.'

I looked at Charity and then at Patience and then at their younger sister Hope. They all bore they same hopeful expression of encouragement. With a sigh, I accepted my fate and gave in.

'Pick me an outfit. Go on.' I also put my hand out, so Patience could put a drink in it.

I hadn't drunk apple sours for years.

By eight o'clock I was on my fifth drink and feeling quite the buzz already. Patience, Hope, and Charity had waited until I accepted defeat and had then stampeded to my bedroom where they proceeded to rip my wardrobe apart.

When they were done, they were good enough to put it all back, but I was left with the slinky, gorgeous and crazy-expensive black dress that Brett had bought me on our weekend in Paris. I told them I didn't want to wear it because of the whole relationship thing with him and in return, I got a lecture about being the woman and not shedding no tears for a man. There was even some finger waggling from the three of them.

Now we were in Bar Nineteen, cleverly named because it was at number nineteen Week Street in Maidstone town centre, and the alcohol was flowing.

There were thirty-two of us in total as several other girls had brought along a friend or friends. One girl had even invited her super-gay brother who was wearing more makeup than any of the girls despite his beard. His gregarious personality and over the top attitude to everything made him an instant hit. Plus, he was some kind of hedge fund analyst in the city or something and was buying all the drinks like it was pocket change.

'Hey, Amanda.' It was Paige, one of the younger police officers at the station.

'Oh, hi, Paige.' She was already tipsy.

'How's the new job going?' She asked.

I said, 'Just fine. I prefer it.' But I could see she had a knowing smile on her face that suggested she didn't want to ask about my job at all. 'What?'

'I saw you on the internet.' She gushed. A couple of the girls standing nearby heard her and turned their attention our way.

191

I merely raised an eyebrow, unsure what she was referring to. She had said it as if she had just discovered I used to make porno videos and had kept it secret all these years.

Paige was fishing her phone from her tiny clutch handbag. A tampon spilled onto the tile as she yanked it free. 'Oops.' She scooped it back into the bag. 'I grew up with four brothers that were into Doctor Who and all that sci-fi stuff and I kinda got hooked on it too.' She was now explaining to a small group as more and more people turned to see what was happening. 'So, I watch an internet show called Alien Quest.'

Bugger.

'There's a really good-looking fellow on it called Jack Hammer and...' she made sure everyone was listening. 'Amanda is the new co-host.'

FFS!

People were congratulating me, even though I was sure most of them had no idea what for. I kept saying that it was a mistake, but no one was hearing me. That was what Paige had meant when she asked me about my new job.

'The bit where you kicked him in the nuts was priceless.' Said Paige. 'Will there be more of that sort of comedy? The show badly needed an injection of entertainment. It looked like you really kicked him too.'

Paige had been fiddling with her phone and had now found the clip she wanted. Faces gathered around the phone, girls near the front scooching down so others at the back could see. Extra faces were joining at the back to see what there was to see, so now we had random men that were in the bar lining up at the back to catch a glimpse. No doubt the men were also propelled by a desire to interact with the horde of ladies in slinky cocktail dresses and this had given them an excuse.

There was near silence in the bar as the clip was replayed. I stood alone on the other side of the phone not wanting to see myself on camera. I heard Jack's voice though and then my own and there was a collective *yay* from the girls and an *oooh* from the men when my foot connected with Jack's spuds.

The footage ended but was replayed over and over by different groups as the crowd watching it through the first time broke into smaller groups for discussion. In some cases, the girls in our group had noticed the boys that had joined us, and pairing was beginning to occur.

'That was quite the show.' I turned to find the super-gay brother whose name I had yet to learn. He was heartachingly pretty in an almost flawless way. He was tall and thin but not skinny. More like an endurance athlete than a gym goer but his skin was radiant and his perfectly even, white teeth showed constantly as he never seemed to stop smiling. His beard was clipped short and like his hair, it appeared to be fresh from the barber's shop. I might have been attracted to him if it were not for the heavy and ornate eye makeup and dark purple lipstick.

'It's not what people think.' I got a quizzical face in return. 'They think I am the co-host for that stupid internet show and the kick was staged. I'm not and it wasn't.'

'Oh, so you did kick him in the nuts, live in front of millions of people?'

'I don't think his viewership extends to millions, but yes.'

'Is there some history there, love?' He asked, a smile teasing the corner of his mouth.

'No!' Urh. The very thought. Jack was such a slime bag.

'Fair enough.' He conceded though I was not sure he believed me. 'I'm Roy. Do you know my sister?'

'Maisy? Yes, I was a police officer until a couple of days ago.'

We chatted briefly about nothing much, then around us, I saw that the girls were gathering their coats and bags. The group was decamping to the club across the street.

The base was pumping inside the walls of the club. We had a VIP area reserved which meant we could abandon our bags and not think about them as the hulking but silent security guy guarding our booth would make sure they were safe. I was left alone in the booth though. All the other girls had shot off, leaving me with a glass of something fizzy and sweet that was supposed to be VIP champagne. I had tasted proper champagne. Brett had a love for it. I caught myself thinking about him. It was a natural thing to do after a breakup, but the truth was, we had barely dated, and we had only slept together a couple of times. Still, he had been fantastic, an utterly wonderful gentleman. If it were not for the baby thing, I might be getting distracted by the displays in the bridal shop windows. I was confused by it all, by my emotions more than anything else. The alcohol had lowered my defences, letting disappointment and weak thoughts sneak in.

Patience bumped against me as she sat down. 'Hey, girl. You see all these fine men? Why aren't you dancing with someone?'

The answer to that question was multi-faceted but was mostly to do with my opinion that no one ever meets anyone in a club. It is impossible to have a conversation over the noise unless one retreats to the quieter bar upstairs and the men came here for hook-ups, not looking for their future significant other. I had no interest in hooking up.

Another big reason why I was sitting in the booth by myself and not mixing was not to do with Brett, but all to do with the alien milk case. There was something there that I was missing. Something about Glen and his wife and the two farmer's wives...

'What's going on inside that big blonde noggin, Amanda?' Patience asked using her serious tone.

'Nothing much. Thinking about life. Thinking about Brett. Thinking about this stupid case and what I am missing.'

'Now is not the time to be blue, Amanda. Everyone is having fun around you. Just stop thinking and enjoy the atmosphere. Answers will come when they are ready.'

I twirled my drink in my fingers, trying to think of something to say.

Patience sat herself up properly and grabbed my free hand. 'Tell me. Explain it in simple terms I can understand, and I will share the burden with you.'

'You would do that, wouldn't you?' Patience was a real friend. Not one that would disappear at the first sign of trouble.

'Of course, sweetie. Sisters share everything.' She took the drink out of my hand and downed it to prove a point. 'Except men. Sisters never share men. That creates all kinds of problems.'

What she had said made me think about the case. 'I have to go.' I told Patience as I grabbed my clutch bag.

She blocked my way. 'Oh no, you don't. Missy, we never go out anymore. You are going to stay here with me and you are going to have a good time. You don't have to get close to no man if you don't want to. You can come dance with me and my sisters. Charity is married, and Hope is saving herself because she wants to be Prime Minister one day and can't have a shady past.'

Patience's face was imploring. I wanted to get home and do research, but she was right, we didn't go out much anymore and I was already here. Was I becoming boring?

Concerned that I was turning into an old spinster, I let Patience take my hand and pull me onto the dance floor where her two sisters were throwing shapes and getting the attention of half a dozen men. To be fair, I think most of the attention was directed toward the tall, athletic and gorgeous Hope, but the men were not making it too overtly obvious.

I promised myself I would stop drinking at that point, so I could have a clear head by the time I got home. I would enjoy a couple of hours out with some friends, get home late for once and then, when I got in, I would sift through the pack of background information James had sent.

I would solve this crime before I got into bed.

A Discovery. Sunday, November 13th 0915hrs

I heard my phone beep. It woke me, although truthfully, I was already mostly awake but electing to remain in bed where I was warm and cozy and didn't have to find out how my head felt. That would happen when I sat up.

The phone beeped again, which it always did if I didn't read the message it had beeped about the first time. I glanced at my clock. It was after nine. I groaned both internally and physically as I tried to remember what had happened.

I could distinctly remember deciding that I was going to stop drinking as I could then come home to do research. We had been dancing... Shots! Someone had shouted for shots and one of the boys we had been talking to, appeared with a tray of them. I had tried to resist... That sounded right.

What had happened then? Clear memories of the night were failing to coalesce. I had woken alone, which was something to be thankful for and as I gazed around the room, I could see my dress hung on the wardrobe door on the little hanger it came with, so I had been alert enough to deal with basic admin tasks when I came in.

Ruefully, I started to get up, moving slowly in anticipation of my head beginning to pound. I had been wearing nothing beneath my dress last night, the dress didn't really allow for it, so it was no surprise that I was naked. I found a small bruise on my left thigh which I had no explanation for but otherwise, I was fine. My head even seemed to be devoid of hangover. I would get some water in me anyway to fight latent dehydration.

Remembering that I showed all I had to Jack and Uncle Knobhead just a couple of days ago, I slipped on a dressing gown before I opened my bedroom door and peeked out. There was no sign of anyone.

I looked about for my phone. Its beep had woken me but now it was silent, and I couldn't find it. My clutch bag was on the kitchen counter, but the phone wasn't in it. I gave up searching and picked up the kettle instead. I made coffee and stood blowing the surface of it. I wanted it to be cool enough to drink.

My phone beeped. I froze, trying to pinpoint where the noise had come from. I knew it would beep again in just a few seconds. I held my breath. The beep came, I spun to face the direction of the noise but still couldn't see it. I started lifting things to look under them and found it next to the oven and under the oven gloves.

What were they doing out?

The message was from Kieron:

Amanda, sorry, things have changed. Your services will no longer be required. Please provide a final bill.

I read it twice, which didn't take long and wondered what had happened. Was he bored with my lack of progress? I was getting somewhere with the case now. I had only been at it for three days after all. I had explained that it would take time to piece it all together. Maybe the milk had gone back to normal? Maybe the culprit had been caught red-handed putting pills into the cows feed.

I called him to at least obtain a clearer picture. I got no answer though. I tried once more with the same result then replied to his text message. A simple question:

Did you solve the case?

While I waited for an answer, I sipped my coffee.

'Do I smell coffee?'

The sudden and unexpected voice made me jump and spill my drink. Patience was on my sofa. She had clearly slept there and was now struggling to lever herself into an upright position.

I had totally forgotten that she had decided to come back to my place last night. Why had that been a good idea?

Then I remembered the pizza. We had been discussing food and as soon as we started talking about it, we were both too hungry to not eat. Everywhere except the greasy kebab place was shut so I had suggested the frozen pizza that I had at home.

That was why the oven gloves were out.

I opened the oven, unsure what I would find. The answer was frozen pizza. Or more accurately, defrosted frozen pizza that was just as cooked as it had been when I put it in there. It hung limply over the bars of the oven shelf at the edges. At least I had taken it out of the packaging even though I hadn't turned the oven on.

I shrugged and cranked the dial on the oven as I closed the door. Pizza for breakfast sounded really good and my stomach gave a growl at the thought.

Patience had managed to get to her feet. Her dress had gotten all turned around as she slept in it, so she was fighting to straighten it out without taking it off.

'I might have drunk too much last night.' She admitted, then yawned deeply, lost her balance as she closed her eyes and fell over.

I flicked the kettle back on to make more coffee.

Just as the clock flicked over to ten o'clock, Patience came out of my bathroom with a towel wrapped around her hair and another around her torso. 'I need bacon.' She announced.

'You just ate half a pizza.' I pointed out.

She raised her eyebrows. 'That little thing? That was barely a snack. It's breakfast time. Patience needs bacon.'

I changed the subject. 'I'm going to the houses of the college kids this morning. You want to see them again?'

'You damned skippy I do. I owe that skinny, little dick a smack in the trousers. Bacon first though.'

'There's some in the fridge.' I looked at the clock. 'Tell you what, I'll make you a bacon sandwich, you dry your hair and get dressed and we'll set off once you have eaten, okay.'

'Fine by me.' Patience flounced into my bedroom as I pulled out my grill and loaded it with bacon rashers.

The hair drier came on as Patience began singing to herself.

Five minutes later I walked the bacon sandwich into my bedroom to find Patience back in her outfit from last night.

'You're going out in that?'

'Patience looked at herself in the mirror. 'Yeah. I look hot.'

It was not the adjective I would have used but I went with it. 'Not exactly the outfit for investigating crime though. Will you be comfortable?'

She slid her feet into four-inch-high heels and stood up. 'It's what I've got. If you want me to change, we need to go via my house for a new outfit.'

I was closing in on the case, but I had plenty to do today without adding in delays and detours. 'You look hot.' I agreed. 'Let's go kick some ass.'

Patience grabbed the sandwich, took a hefty bite from it and let her eyes roll back in a display of ecstasy.

Thirty minutes later I stopped the car in front of 54 Hopkirk Drive in Twydall. It was just before eleven o'clock on a Sunday morning in a pleasingly well-tended housing estate. The houses were all detached with garages and neat front lawns. There were lots of trees and the cars parked on driveways were mostly new. The ones that weren't new were most likely the property of teenage children. It looked like a nice place to live.

The driveway of the house had a fifteen-year-old French-made P.O.S. car on it that had to belong to Christian Rogers. This was the house of his mother. A fast check this morning had revealed the father had absconded some years ago.

Patience accompanied me to the front door which was answered before I could knock. The woman inside was in a business suit and heels with a briefcase under her arm. She looked like a lawyer. We caught her by surprise as she was clearly opening the door to leave, not because she had seen us.

'Oh!' She exclaimed. 'You gave me a fright. Sorry I was just leaving.'

She looked the pair of us up and down. If she thought Patience's outfit choice for this time on a Sunday was odd, then she kept it to herself. Patience flashed her police ID. Since she had it with her it seemed the simplest way of getting the woman's attention.

'Mrs. Rogers?' I asked.

'Yes.'

'Is Christian home?'

The question seemed to catch her off guard. 'Has he done something?'

Patience spoke, 'That's what we hope to find out.'

'What do you know about his dealing with crop circles?' I asked.

The woman was hovering, half in and half out of her door, keys in one hand and briefcase still tucked under her arm. Until I asked that question, she had looked like she was going to push through us at any second. Now she sagged. 'I knew it. I knew that device would cause problems.'

'What device?' Patience and I asked simultaneously.

Mrs. Rogers led us to her garage. Before she opened it though she put her briefcase down on the old French car and used the key to plip open a Mercedes across the street. 'I haven't been able to park it in my garage for six months. He said he had an idea for an invention and, as a mother does, I supported him and even gave him some money for parts he said he needed to buy.'

She was opening the garage door with a key as she talked. The handle turned with a squeak of protest, then the door swung upward to vanish into the ceiling. Inside was an odd looking… Vehicle? I wasn't sure what to call it. It looked like a ride-on lawn mower with the seat removed. Beneath it, where the wheels should be, was a rubber apron.

'He makes crop circles with it.' Mrs. Rogers explained.

Patience and I looked at each other, then went in for a closer look. Behind us, Mrs. Rogers was muttering about the boy never tidying up, never helping out, etcetera. Her biggest gripe was that she had to park her car in the street like a peasant.

I ignored her as I inspected the device.

'Mum! What are you doing?'

My head snapped up to see Christian in an ill-fitting pair of jogging bottoms and pair of slippers. He was naked from the waist up, his pale skin complementing his skinny frame perfectly.

'What have I told you about wearing your slippers outside of the house?' Mrs. Rogers demanded.

He stared at her. Then waved his arm at Patience and me. 'Bigger concerns right now, mum.'

I had a question for him, 'What is this, Christian? Someone has written *Crop Circler 5000* on it with a black marker.'

He gawped at me, then at Patience and then at his mother. He was caught, and he knew it.

'Do you need me?' Mrs. Rogers asked.

'Is your son eighteen?' Patience asked.

'Yes, he is.' She replied happily, understanding the implication. 'Good luck, Christian. It's about time you started taking responsibility.' She picked up her briefcase and went to her car without a backward glance.

Christian was twitching on the spot, clearly unsure what his next move was. He was also getting cold and he wasn't the only one.

'Shall we go inside and have a chat and a cup of tea, Christian?' I suggested.

It didn't take long to get the full story. The device was hand-built in his mum's garage by Christian and Lee using parts they reclaimed from scrap yards mostly. They had to buy some of the electronic components as the crop circler was radio-controlled. It was a giant radio-controlled hovercraft.

They were art students. They had one lecturer they wanted to impress after he set them a tough assignment about naturally forming art. The assignment carried points for the final grade, but while their fellow students had been looking at patterns on butterflies or birds or in rocks, the two boys had hit upon the idea of crop circles. Their intricate spiral designs were unexplained by nature or man but had a beautiful symmetry to them. They were required to find live examples though, which was impossible if one didn't know where a crop circle might appear. The phenomenon was also far rarer than it had been a decade before and there had never been a crop circle in Kent, so they would have to travel if they heard about one.

The plan to make their own arose. Christian had proudly boasted that they had scored an A and got a special mention by the lecturer for their originality. When Patience and I had appeared at their college, the two boys had been terrified we would reveal the truth and they would be ejected from the Master's program with their Bachelors qualifications rescinded.

I felt like I should lecture the boy about cheating, but I was mostly glad to have solved a piece of the case and to have found it was in no way related to the milk or the lights or the spacecraft. Instead of a lecture, I thanked Christian for being candid. I did say that it might be best if he dismantled the crop circler now and forever keep quiet about it, but then there was nothing else I needed to say, and it was time to leave.

I checked my phone. Still no reply from Kieron. I called his number again – still no answer. I had a voice in my head telling me I could just go home now, put my feet up and have the day off. Something wasn't right though, and I wanted to hear from Kieron why he felt the case no longer needed solving.

If the baby had come, they would still be at the hospital so that was where I was going.

We told the lady on the post-natal reception desk that we were friends of Lara Fallon and were instantly rewarded with her room number.

I believed it to be highly probable that Kieron was here, that I would push open the door to their room and find him sitting next to his wife as they cooed over their brand-new baby. Even if he wasn't, and ignoring the bit where Lara seemed to loathe the sight of me, I was sure I would be able to learn from her what had changed with the case.

I was wrong though, very wrong. As I gently pushed open the door and saw Lara nursing her baby, I understood just how wrong I had been. Not just about finding Kieron but about everything, and the case turned on its head again.

The tiny infant clinging to her chest had black, curly hair and beautiful, chocolate brown skin.

Patience shoved into the room because I had frozen halfway through the door when I had seen the child. She froze beside me, but in contrast to my silent observation as Lara grimaced, Patience had something to say, 'That white girl has a brown baby.' She observed with a chuckle.

I had just one thought: It's Glen's. With that everything slotted into place.

I turned to leave the room and bumped into Patience. 'We have to go. I have to check something right now.'

I was out the door and running back along the corridor. The thing that had been itching away at the back of my head had just surfaced. I had seen the evidence, the connection I couldn't find. It was in the pack of information Jane had pulled together at the start of the case.

My pulse was racing as I skidded to a stop at my car and yanked the door open. 'Come on, Patience!' I yelled. She was hurrying but it was more of a sashay than a jog.

She was out of breath anyway. 'What the hell is going on, Amanda?' She puffed as she flopped into my car.

'I think I know who did it and why.'

'Who, why, what? Slow down, girl.'

I left the car park, heading for town. I needed to drop Patience off and get home. On the way, I explained my thoughts, 'The milk. I was originally hired to find out what was causing the milk to glow. I think they might have hired someone else, like a normal PI, if it were not for the crop circles and the aliens and all the weird lights at night. I have been trying to find the mastermind orchestrating it all, or at least I had been until yesterday when I decided it had to be Jack pretending to be the Alien. If he is guilty of that bit and the crop circles are nothing more than art class homework, then all I am actually trying to solve is the milk.'

'Who stands to gain. That is the question I started with, but there seemed to be no one involved that would benefit from the farms going under. I wondered if the farm manager, Gordon McIntosh might be to blame but I reckon I am about to rule him out.'

'So, who is it?' Patience asked.

'I need to check something first, but if I am right, we have a murderer to catch and maybe another killing to stop. Get your uniform on and get to the farms.'

'Righto.' Patience was happy to just accept my request.

'One more thing.'

'Yeah?'

'How many of the sniffer dog guys do you know?' I asked.

She thought for a second. 'All of them, I think.'

Okay. 'How many of them do you know well.'

Patience grinned at me. 'All of them.'

She was such a slut.

'Well, we need a favour. Can you call it in?' I explained my thoughts and let her make a phone call as we sped toward her house.

I didn't even shut my front door as I ran to my kitchen counter to open my laptop. As it booted up, I dialled Jane's number and prayed she would answer on a Sunday.

'Hi, Amanda.' Her deep voice came on the phone.

'Jane.' I had urgency in my voice. 'I need your expertise. Are you near a computer?'

'I will be in about three seconds.' There was a pause. 'Okay, shoot.'

I told her what to look for and what it meant and left her to get on with it. As the phone clicked off, the image I wanted to see finished loading and displayed on my laptop.

The mystery hoody had told me to look at a university photograph. An unhelpful cryptic clue which only made sense now. He hadn't meant the photograph of Kieron and Richard. He meant Lara and Michelle. I sent the picture to the printer, grabbed my bag and phone and legged it back to my car.

As I drove, I listened to Kieron's phone ringing. I was seriously concerned that I might not get to the farms in time, but he wasn't going to answer. I tried the number for Glen but he didn't answer either. I swore in my frustration, then, as I left the main road and went out into the countryside, I drove faster.

The call from Jane came ten minutes before I got to the farm. She had found more than I expected. And the truth was more surprising than I could have anticipated.

Farm Fight. Sunday, November 13th 1254hrs

I had no idea which farm I needed to go to. I had worked out most of it in my head, but I still had missing bits left unanswered. I wanted to find Kieron, but he was still not answering his phone, so I was going to his farm to see if I could catch him there. He might not be on any of the farms, of course. With his wife delivering a baby that was most certainly not his, he might have just got in his car and driven towards the sunset.

I was driving fast, unsure of what I would find when I arrived. It would more likely be something than nothing, I was sure of that.

It turned out to be something all right.

As I whipped my little car up the path the led to the farm, I saw a scene unfolding in front of me. A dozen farm hands were standing motionless as Kieron threatened Glen with a shotgun. Richard and Michelle were there too, off to one side not far from their car.

I skidded to a stop and leaped out. 'Kieron, wait!' I shouted.

His head twitched in my direction but nothing more.

Behind me, a taxi pulled to a stop. I had shot by it less than a minute ago to a blast of horn just outside Cliffe Woods village. Kieron's head might be facing toward me now but his eyes weren't. They were on the cab. His wife Lara was getting out of it with her baby.

'Kieron don't.' She cried out.

He turned his gaze back towards Glen and pulled the shotgun tighter into his shoulder. If he pulled the trigger there would be no doubt about the result. Glen was twenty feet away. At that range, the weapon would cut him in half.

I watched as Kieron gritted his teeth. Richard twitched forward, 'Take it easy, Kieron. Let's not do something rash.'

'Stay out of it, Richard.' He warned. 'This doesn't concern you.'

210

'Actually, I rather think it might.' I was adopting my cop voice. The one that insisted authority. The one I had never been very good at.

'Just shut up and stay out of it.' Snapped Lara.

I needed to keep Kieron calm. Find a way to disarm him. 'Kieron, this is all recoverable.'

'Oh, yeah? How are you going to fix my baby, Amanda?' His voice was strained with emotion as he shouted his reply.

Well, apart from that bit. I thought.

I tried again. 'Kieron if you kill him you will go to jail. Nothing will stop that from happening. But if you don't kill him, he will be going to jail.'

Kieron's eyebrow lifted in question. 'I'm listening.'

I could hear another car coming up the path toward the farm behind me. Unwilling to take my eyes off the situation in front of me, I assumed it was Patience arriving with the cavalry. Uniforms at the scene would halt his murderous intentions. I couldn't blame him for going nuts. I might do the same in his situation.

A car door shut and feet hit the gravel behind me as they crunched toward me and stopped by my shoulder.

'Well, this is entertaining.' Said Jack bloody Hammer. It wasn't Patience at all.

I held up a warning finger to silence him, my eyes still locked on Kieron. 'Kieron, I know what is making the milk glow and I know why.'

Glen twitched, his eyes on me rather than the business end of the shotgun now.

Michelle grabbed Richard's arm. 'Come on, Richard. I've seen enough if this.' She tried to tug him away, he just looked at her confused.

'What's happening?' He asked. The question was aimed at anyone that wanted to field it.

'You really don't know, Richard?' I asked, my voice filled with mock surprise. 'Kieron, I would really like you to put the shotgun down before I tell you what I have discovered. The police are on their way. Even if the guilty parties run, they will not get far.'

'I have had enough of this nonsense.' Lara was making determined steps toward her farmhouse.

Even though I saw it coming, the blast from the shotgun stunned me. The quiet of the farm was split as a single barrel roared. Kieron had aimed it in the air and wasted half of his two shots. The point had been made though. Lara was frozen to the spot.

'Stay. Where. You. Are. Lara.' The words came out through clenched teeth. 'Keep talking please, Amanda. You said guilty parties, as in plural. How many of my friends are involved?' He moved his shotgun between Glen and Lara and then swung it toward Richard and Michelle.

Each of them looked terrified.

I took a step toward him. For his own good, I might need to tackle him or try to take the weapon from him before he could use it. I started talking as I began to edge nearer. 'Do you remember that Glen's father's farm was confiscated?' He nodded. 'Well, it ended up under government control alright, but only after Glen sold it to them for millions after he found natural gas beneath it.'

'That's not true!' Glen shouted. His reaction caused the shotgun to swing back towards him, an action that elicited his silence once more.

'I have a friend that is surprisingly good at finding details, Glen. This is all quite easy to prove.'

'That's very interesting.' Said Michelle. 'But what does it have to do with our milk?'

I ignored the question as I pressed on. 'The first clue was the university photograph of the sisters.'

'What sisters?'

'I'm glad you asked, Kieron. Your wife is Michelle's sister.'

Michelle chuckled. 'Preposterous.'

'Oh, really, Michelle? A friend of mine said something yesterday that stuck with me. It didn't mean anything at the time. Shall I tell you what she said?' I let the question hang as I looked around at my audience.

'Well, I want to know.' Said Jack from behind me.

Quelling an almost overwhelming urge to kick him in the trousers again, I said, 'Sisters share everything. Except for men.'

'Wonderful.' Sniped Lara. 'I'll have a bumper sticker made.'

'Lara, why don't you show Michelle your baby?'

She froze at my suggestion.

'What does she mean, Lara?' Asked Michelle.

Lara had nothing to say, but I did. It wasn't about Lara and her baby though. 'I got caught up investigating Glen and Tamara. I found out that the substance that is making the milk glow is the same bioluminescent stuff that makes cuttlefish glow. It is used in medicine, so I figured Tamara the pharmacist had supplied it in sufficient quantities to dope the herds. But she couldn't administer it to all three farms at once so there had to be other people involved. And the herds were continuing to produce luminous milk even after she died.'

Michelle was trying to see the baby Lara had tucked into her chest.

'The milk was white again this morning wasn't it, Kieron?'

'How could you know that?' He asked.

'It was a guess actually, but one based on deductive reasoning. The university photograph I mentioned earlier had the two girls, Lara and Michelle in their graduating class at Dorchester University. Also in the picture, is Glen Adongo. He was on secondment from Southampton University at the time. Isn't that right, Glen?'

Glen didn't answer, but Richard had a question. For his wife. 'What does she mean, Michelle? Is Lara your sister?' This confirmed something I had been wondering about.

I carried on telling my story, 'There is a bit here that I cannot prove. A bit that is part conjecture and part anecdote. The girls had other friends at university. The photograph helpfully named them all. When my colleague spoke to some of them this morning, they claimed that Glen was sleeping with Michelle. I imagine the two of them kept it very hush, hush though.'

'Why is that?' Asked Jack helpfully.

Lara was looking utterly panicked now.

'Because he was also sleeping with her sister, Lara.'

'No!' Screamed Michelle. 'He's mine, Lara. He was always mine.'

'What the hell are you saying, Michelle?' Asked Richard, his world unravelling before his eyes.

Kieron didn't know where to point the weapon. I moved a pace closer.

'Show me that baby!' Michelle demanded.

'I don't believe this!' Richard was burying his face in his hands.

Kieron said, 'Looks like they got us both, buddy.' He thought he had one friend left, but he was wrong about that too.

'Not so fast there, Kieron.'

'Huh?'

'I'm afraid the greatest betrayal of all, might be Richard's.'

Richard's eyes were out on stalks. 'But I helped you.' He pleaded.

All too late, I thought as I pressed on once more. 'Richard discovered, by accident I assume, that there is natural gas beneath the soil here. It doesn't really matter how he came about the information, because it was

214

Richard that went looking for a Geologist last year. He found Glen, Glen checked it out and between them, they cooked up a plan to get your farm out from under you.'

'It wasn't like that.' Richard protested. 'I wanted to tell you, mate. You were just so set on being a farmer here and struggling along. We could have made a fortune and set up again somewhere else without all the debt and worry. It would have been so brilliant.'

'I even remember you telling me something about it. About natural gas on the land.' Kieron admitted, his face still a mask of anger.

'Yes, that's right. I told you about it straight away.'

'And I said I would rather die than have the beautiful countryside ripped up just to get at some gas. Fracking would have destroyed the land.' With the shotgun now pointing toward Richard because that was where Kieron was facing, Glen tried to take a step backward. 'Don't you move.' Kieron instructed quietly. The stillness and calm in his voice scarier than the weapon at this point.

'I was going to share the money with you, Kieron.' Richard was pleading. 'Both of us together with the girls and the babies would have flourished, free of debt and money worries at new farms.'

I needed to interject. 'Except you wouldn't have. Would they, Glen?' All eyes swung to me. 'Your wives were never yours, Richard. Both belong to another man. They seduced you on his instruction. He was going to have all the land once you were bankrupt. Maybe he even planned to fake your suicides. I can only imagine how deep this goes, but tell me, Richard, do you have a large freezer on your property anywhere?'

He didn't answer, but Michelle's expression told me I had scored another hit.

'It is where Glen and Michelle stashed Tamara's body when he killed her. Why did you kill her, Glen?'

What was keeping Patience? Where was she?

I was taking my time, but I didn't know how long I could string this out. 'Was it that she found out about Michelle? Or Lara? Or both of them? Or was it something else? Did she find out that you had been using her contacts to get hold of the pills you were doping the cows with? Or was she in on it and changed her mind?'

'It was an accident.' Glen blurted, speaking for the first time in minutes.

'An accident.' I repeated. 'You called Michelle though and shoved Tamara's body in the freezer at Richard's farm. Who came up with the genius idea to plant her body outside when you heard about the alien?'

No one answered for a moment, then Lara broke the silence and finally the confession started. 'It was her idea.' She said, pointing to Michelle while cradling the baby with her other arm. 'She always wanted Tamara dead.'

'Lara, what are you saying?' Shrieked Michelle, but it sounded fake.

'Tamara caught Glen kissing me and went nuts. She was in on the whole thing but had no idea either of us was sleeping with her husband. That bitch was so blind. Just like you Michelle, you wanted Glen for yourself. We could have shared him, but you always pretended you didn't know.'

'I didn't know!' She shouted.

'Ladies, there is enough of me to go around. We can still be a happy family.' Glen's comment drew stares from Richard and Kieron.

The shotgun came back around to point at Glen's head. 'You better start talking or I'm going to blow your head off.' Kieron promised.

Nervously, Glen raised his hands in surrender, but he started talking. 'There is a huge pocket of natural gas beneath your feet. Tens of millions of pounds, maybe even more than that. We own the land, Kieron. All we have to do is agree to extract it and we are all richer than you can count.'

'I don't give a damn about the gas. Why is my wife holding your baby?'

216

'I needed you to be distracted and to feel safe. I needed to know what you were doing. Lara and Michelle agreed to seduce and marry you both so the three of us could gain control of the land. Lara was never meant to get pregnant.'

'The three of us.' I echoed. All eyes turned to me. 'Your plan never included Tamara, did it? Were you always going to kill her?'

'I had a dead body in my freezer.' Richard was borderline catatonic. He was burbling to himself and cradling his face.

'Hold on. Hold on.' Demanded Kieron. 'What about the milk? You knew that my milk was back to normal this morning. How?'

'Because Lara hadn't been here to put fresh dope into their feed. Glen and Richard and Tamara and Michelle and Lara were all in this wonderful little plot together. Glen was the geologist that could test and confirm the potential size and worth of the find. Richard was the well-meaning idiot, who, by the way, did a top job of trying to help me solve the case by dressing up in a hoody and a mask and feeding me clues.' Richard's jaw hung slack. He clearly believed I would not work out it was him. 'Richard got cold feet and wanted to expose the truth, so he fed me clues but tried to conceal his identity. He pointed me toward a picture of the girls at Uni, hoping I would spot Glen and make the connection. He didn't know the girls were sisters and certainly didn't know that his wife was never on his side.' I made eye contact with Richard. 'It that your baby she carries?' His horrified face turned to stare at his wife's belly.

'Lara and Michelle are the poisonous sisters that would marry and sleep with a man just to ensure they could manipulate his actions. That's why Lara has been pushing you to sell. Glen has money from the sale of his father's farm. My friendly researcher had difficulty proving that bit as finances are always well hidden. He got there though. Glen would have bought the land and then done whatever he wanted. He couldn't just do it on his own land because it would tip his hand to you. He wanted it all. That's how the greedy mind works. It always wants more.'

'The girls were doping the cows. None of the farm hands would question the farmer's wife going into the milking shed to see the cows each morning, now would they?'

Kieron saw the truth of it. Then his brow knitted again. 'What about the alien Lara saw?'

'Oh, that was real.'

'What?' He squeaked.

'Well, it was really there. But it was this man,' I grabbed Jack by his shoulder, 'inside a suit. He was taking advantage of the recent crop circles, which by the way were an art project made by Lee and Christian, the two college geeks you met, and the report of glowing milk and the lights reported in the sky.' Beside me Jack was smiling broadly as he shook his head. 'It was all a ruse to advance his show.'

'Oh, Amanda. You could not be more wrong if you tried.'

'It worked too, didn't it, Jack? You are suddenly quite famous.'

The blissful sound of sirens in the distance reached my ears. I was just about to tell them about the lights in the sky when the tension that had been keeping everyone in place finally broke.

Hearing the police on their way, Glen, knowing he was guilty of murder, ran for it. Kieron reacted by swinging the shotgun to fire at Glen's back.

I shouted for him to stop, but I couldn't get to him before the gun went off.

Michelle meanwhile had crossed the yard to confront her sister. Lara was defending her baby as Michelle ranted and screamed at her. Richard didn't move.

But Kieron's shot mostly missed Glen. There was a shout of pain, but Glen ducked around the side of the farm and was gone.

'Nobody move.' I commanded.

218

Nobody listened though. I turned to wave to the police cars as they were sweeping into the farm. Leading the way was Patience with the terrified face of Brad Hardacre in the passenger seat.

Officers spilled from the cars and vans to separate the sisters and to cuff Richard and Kieron. Kieron was still holding the shotgun and looking beaten.

The sound of a quad bike preceded Glen emerging from behind a barn astride it. He shot off across the field over terrain the police vehicles were not suited to.

They were not defeated for long though, two Land Rovers were requisitioned in seconds, Patience once again trying to get behind the wheel only to find no one was brave enough to get in with her.

Quiet had fallen at the farm. Glen had been chased and caught. Everyone was under arrest and evidence was being gathered. Soon they would take Glen, Richard, and the girls away. Kieron was being questioned but was not in cuffs as he was considered to be the victim.

His farm was safe, he could return to making a living, but I doubted he would ever feel the same about it again. He was sitting on top of a fortune in natural energy yet had principles that denied him the option of getting to it. Without it though, and without the other farms to support his milk producing efforts, would he even be able to stay in business?

These were not my concerns. My concern was that I had a bill for the last few days and I had to hand it to a man that I knew to be not only broke but broken-spirited and broken-hearted as well.

It could wait.

I was getting hungry. Lunch simply hadn't happened. I wandered outside to see if the police had some food going.

I spotted Jack. He was lounging against a fence looking like he hadn't a care in the world. What on earth was he doing here anyway? Today's revelations had done nothing to further his cause. He had reported in the Supernatural Times that the milk was aliens attempting to subvert humankind. Today's revelations disproved his theories. I still hadn't confronted him about that.

Well, I was going to do it now. Let's see what effect that had on his smug grin.

'There's an alien spacecraft over Larson Farm!'

All eyes turned to the voice. A farm worker was holding his mobile phone and shouting. In the quiet, we could just about make out the voice on his speaker.

'Barry sent me a picture of it. It just scared the herd over by east field. Now it's heading through the woods toward Hogget's Hill.'

No one moved.

'He says there's an alien as well. Soldiers are hunting it.'

All around me, people exploded into action. Farm hands were jumping onto anything with wheels and a motor. The police that were not directly involved with sweeping up the events at Brompton farm piled into their cars.

Next to me, as I fiddled with my bag to find my keys, Jack said, 'Well, well. I appear to be standing here next to you. I hope you will let me help you with wardrobe when we present together. Something revealing ought to fit the bill. Nothing slutty, just enough skin to tease though.'

I shoved him roughly out of my way as I ran to my car. The farmhands were going cross country, the roads would be faster, but where the police would need to navigate, I already knew where I was going.

I had a bad feeling about the alien. If soldiers were indeed chasing it, they must be from BARF. I had a hunch BARF were not a government-sanctioned unit at all, but instead a privately funded bunch of morons. Would they be armed? I shuddered to think.

I mashed my foot down as I came out of the farm and onto what passed for a main road in the countryside. Hogget's farm was three miles away through twisting country lanes. I had to be the first to get there though.

If I had the map right in my head, the alien was heading north through the woods that bordered the upper edge of Larson Farm. The woods ended at a road where the creature would have to emerge to continue onwards.

With my car whipping along the tight roads as fast as I dared to push it and a constant prayer for tractors to stay in the field on my lips, I spied ahead of me the deep crimson and black of a BARF vehicle. As I drew nearer, I could make out the distinctive shape of a Land Rover Defender.

I had a police car behind me in which I could see Patience and Brad Hardacre with grim faces as they tried to keep up with me. Brad was at the wheel and giving it all he had, but the mini was simply better engineered for this kind of driving. I caught the BARF truck and went directly around it, risking my life to get through a tiny gap before we hit the next corner.

Patience and Brad got stuck behind it. That was what I needed though. I had to be the one to intercept the alien and I had to be alone.

More corners at dangerous speeds and suddenly I was there. I hit the brake pedal and skidded to a stop, my tyres skipping across the road and leaving rubber behind.

I spotted the alien instantly. It had already crossed the road and was running across the scrubby field to the north. The only feature ahead of it was Hogget's Hill. In the open, it was massively exposed.

A shout brought my attention around to look the way the alien had just come. Through the woods to the south, I could see guys in uniform. The same deep crimson and black, which did little to camouflage them in the woods as they were darker than everything else. I wondered if they were armed until a shot rang out.

Panicked, I pulled out my mobile phone, scrolled through my contact list and pressed dial.

The alien faltered mid-run. I was right.

I honked my horned and waved out the window. The alien was one hundred yards away to the north. The soldiers in the woods were less than that to the south and they had not only seen the alien, not hard in its daft silver suit but had seen me as well.

Another shot rang out and this time I saw a puff of grass pop into the air ten feet to the left of the alien.

With no option, I turned my wheel and drove the mini off the road while praying the recent rain hadn't made the ground boggy.

Behind me, the BARF truck came around the corner, with Brad right behind it, giving some horn in protest.

The poor Mini wasn't designed to go cross-country. I wasn't sure what the best tactic was, but I knew I didn't want to stop, and I didn't want to weave around much.

I was going slow though, just trying to keep my wheels moving. The alien was coming toward me, the distance closing fast. I powered down the window and yelled for it to jump with all the volume I could muster.

I had turned so I was parallel with it, so it could run along beside me and dive in headfirst. With a distinctly human lack of grace, that was what it did. We were still moving, the upside-down alien flailing around and knocking my arms as I tried to protect myself from its feet. I pointed the car back toward the road and tried to stay ahead of the BARF truck as it barrelled along the far smoother tarmac.

I got the mini back to the edge of the grass and regained the road. Not a moment too soon as the BARF truck was bearing down on me. I stomped on the gas pedal to get away, then saw another vehicle with BARF markings coming toward me from the other direction and yet more vehicles behind that. They were being pursued by more police cars though, the sound of sirens now everywhere.

Frustrated soldiers were emerging from the woods to my left and would be on the road and in my way in seconds if I didn't floor it. They were pointing their weapons at me but none of them fired because the alien was still upside down with its head stuck in the footwell and its feet flailing.

I could see just one chance. Ahead of me, there was a turning, it looked like a track, rather than a road. Something you might take a horse down, but I needed to get the alien away from the crazy BARF nutters that might shoot without questioning what was inside the suit and away from the police, as they would undoubtedly ask too many questions.

The mini leaped forward, its sporty little engine leaving the slow-moving BARF Land Rover and the soldiers in its wake but creating a game of chicken with those coming toward me. I needed to go faster if I was going to make it.

Adrenalin was making my pulse race. I felt slightly sick and a bit lightheaded as I gritted my teeth against the terror headed my way. I was the smallest car in this equation. Get it wrong and I might not survive the crash.

Then a shot rang out to redouble my desire to escape.

With the convoy of BARF military vehicles filling my windscreen, I had to brake to make the turn and only got through because the driver bearing down on me, who got so close I could see his eye colour, realised that if he didn't brake he was going to hit the vehicle chasing me.

I had left my own deceleration just a moment too late, so as I two-wheeled it around the corner, my back end drifted out, slipped off the gravel track and threatened to flip me. Then, just when I thought my teeth were going to shatter I was clenching them so hard, the front-wheel-drive tyres gripped the surface of the track to propel the car onward and I was gone.

In my rear-view, I could see the BARF vehicles all screech to a juddering stop as they fought to follow me and caused a block at the entrance to the track. I reached another turning as the track went into some woods and saw, with my final glance, that the police were swarming over the BARF nutters. They had been running around the woods shooting weapons that were most likely not licensed firearms. There was going to be a stack of arrests.

I powered the window back up.

In the calm quiet of the cab, the alien had righted itself. I could hear its heavy, out of breath gasps of air through its suit.

I allowed my shoulders to relax. We were safe. 'Seatbelt please, Uncle.'

I waited in the dark for over an hour. Just as I was beginning to get a numb bottom and starting to worry that I might have guessed wrong, I heard the sound of a car pull up outside.

Jane had once again been able to find the information I wanted only moments after I had asked it. She always said the internet could tell you anything so long as you knew how to ask. In this case, I had asked her to find property rented under a certain name. It had taken her no time at all to prove that my guess was correct.

I stayed still, waiting for the door to open.

I had gained entry using a set of lock picks, the first time I had ever used such a tool. Tempest had a set at the office, but they were harder to use than they seem in the movies which had forced me to utilise a YouTube tutorial after fifteen minutes of fruitless fiddling.

I wasn't sure if he would be alone or not. There was a distinct danger he might have his accomplice with him, but I was willing to run that risk.

I had taken the precaution of already filming all the evidence in the lockup and sending it to Tempest via email.

A shaft of light from outside illuminated the space inside as the door opened. I had been sitting in darkness for long enough that my eyes had adjusted. The bright glare from the floodlights outside caused me to blink.

He came through the door and flicked on the lights. Illumination spread across the lockup, at the same time bringing light and creating shadows.

I stayed still and watched as he crossed to the roller door. It was an old manual door that required the user to hoist and lower the door using a chain. He unhooked the chain and pulled the door open.

'I'll give you a hand, Bob.' Said Jack as he went outside to help.

I stepped out of the shadow I had been standing in but didn't say anything. Instead, I filmed on my phone as the two men wheeled the spaceship back into the lockup. Up close, it was easy to see that the spaceship was a modified microlight aircraft. It was covered in sheets of what appeared to be carbon fibre that shimmered with iridescence under the halogen bulbs. It was shaped to look nothing like a microlight, so from the sky, or from a distance it would look like an alien spacecraft. Likewise, the alien's spacesuit looked good from a distance, but up close one could see how man-made it was. The cast from the boot matched exactly the bottom of the boots sat next to the suit. They were large rubber wellingtons boots onto which an oversize foot had been moulded.

I had to admire his ingenuity and wondered if the suit itself had come from an old sci-fi movie or TV series. Maybe one that got cancelled or was never aired. It felt highly probable that costumes and props would be made for failed shows and were then sold off for pennies when the budget got cut.

Nevertheless, the ruse was over. I tossed the odd metal component I had found in the woods onto the concrete in front of them.

It made a terrible clanging sound that reverberated off the walls in the silence, causing Jack to jump and Bob to clutch his chest as his heart restarted.

'Did you wonder why your burner stopped working?' I asked.

When I arrived an hour ago, I had taken the grand tour of all the fun artefacts I had found inside. One of them was an industrial weed burner with a big circular steel ring attached to the burner end. The ring looked like a giant cookie cutter and I didn't need to measure it to know that it had been used to contain the flames so Jack could make the twelve rings Fred had found in the woods. A spring hanging out of the device showed where the lever arm, for that was what it was, was supposed to fit.

For the first time since I met him, Jack was without comment.

I crossed the floor to stop right in front of Jack's face. He was able to look down at me but there was no mistaking that I had the upper hand.

'Worried Jack?' I asked. 'You should be. I already filmed all these props. I can expose you and your show. You took advantage of the odd occurrences in Cliffe Woods and added to them. Scaring people and interfering with a police investigation.'

He swallowed. 'What are you going to do?'

I stared directly into his eyes. I had him, and he knew it. 'I'm going to watch your show, Jack.'

'Huh?'

'You set my uncle as bait. To prove I was wrong and that you were not behind all the alien sightings, you had him dress up and cover for you. He thinks all the alien nonsense is real and he thinks you might actually give him a shot on your show, so he did what you asked and put himself in danger. For you. FOR YOU!' I roared.

'Um.'

'Shut up, Jack.' My voice had returned to normal volume. 'It was Bob in the microlight, wasn't it?'

He nodded.

'You are going to get back on the air, Jack and you are going to make your show as successful as you can, and you are going to do it with your co-host Norbert.'

He opened his mouth to protest but seeing my expression he closed it again.

'I will do nothing with the footage I have, provided you pay him a fair wage, let's say thirty percent of profits.' Jack's eyes popped out. 'Does that sound fair to you, Bob?'

'Yeah, thirty percent sounds about right.' Bob replied, suddenly forgetting his coronary distress at the thought of money.

'Thirty percent to each of your team still leaves forty percent to you, Jack. Or nothing. Take your pick.'

With no choice at all, Jack agreed, and I went home to rest. It had been an odd case.

The next show had gone on air the following Saturday, with Norbert Nichols getting almost equal air time. He did well too. Better than I had expected.

Uncle Knobhead had finally found something he might not make a mess of.

Gordon handed me my cup of tea and took a seat opposite me in his small living room. Sitting next to him was his wife Geraldine. His abrasive nature had made me trepidatious about knocking on his door this evening.

I had a final part of the mystery to deal with, so even though I was not being paid to solve this element of it, I wanted to do for my own satisfaction.

Gordon McIntosh's attitude and demeanour were entirely different here though than they had been whenever we had spoken on the farm. Whether it was his wife's influence on him, the impact of recent events, or just that he was under no pressure in his home environment I couldn't tell.

Whatever the case, he was charming and pleasant now.

'Do you believe you will be able to buy the farm?' I asked. Gordon had sensed the impending failure of the farm co-operative and had been preparing for it. His meeting with the bank had been to secure a loan against Wendle farm if it came up for sale. He had investors lined up and a grand plan to raise ostriches for meat and llamas for wool.

'I think so, yes. Mr. Fallon was very interested in my ideas when we sat down earlier today. That's not why you came though, is it? On the phone, you said something about lights in the sky.'

'That's right. You are part of a Falklands war re-enactment team, yes?'

He took a slurp of his tea. 'Indeed. We meet twice a week.'

'On Tuesdays and Thursdays, right?'

'That's right.' Replied his wife as Gordon had his cup to his lips again. 'Are you interested in battle re-enactment?'

'Not exactly. You were a helicopter pilot, so can I assume that your role in the re-enactment is to fly a model helicopter?'

'I didn't give you enough credit, miss. You are quite astute. There are three of us that fly the helicopters, it's devilish hard though, much harder than flying the real thing because you have to do it from the land and judge where each of them is in relation to the others. In the battle for Goose Green, we came in over the coast to drop supplies and report on enemy troop movement.'

'And you have been practising at night over the land near Hogget's Hill.' It was a statement because I had already worked it out.

The war re-enactment bunch might be an odd lot, but not so strange as those that saw the light on the back of the helicopters and thought it was a spaceship. As we chatted and I finished my tea, I listened to Gordon and his wife and their hopes for the future of Wendle Farm. They hadn't bought it yet. It wasn't even up for sale and I had to admit I didn't understand what happened to property when the owners went to jail and couldn't pay the bills.

Clearly, Gordon understood the process, but I didn't take much in when he was explaining it to me. I was too busy thinking about how convoluted the plot had been to swindle Kieron out of his farm and how unnecessary. Richard and Glen could have taken the gas from their land with Kieron unable to stop them. For that matter, Glen didn't need to go to the extremes of putting two women into play as the hapless farmer's wives. Why they had gone along with it I would never know.

They were all in jail with their fate to be determined by a judge. I only felt sorry for the baby.

Patience had called on Sunday evening to tell me how they had arrested forty-three armed civilians led by a retired Brigadier. BARF was not a government organisation but had presented themselves as one to the community of crazies that paid attention to alien conspiracy theories. I guess if you can believe an alien race want to tamper with our milk, then a secret arm of the British Army which specialises in monitoring the alien threat is hardly a leap at all.

When my tea was drunk, and Gordon had explained his plans for the farm, I thanked him and his wife for their hospitality, wished them luck and went back to my car.

It was dark in the countryside as I drove back from Cliffe Woods toward the sprawling Medway Towns ahead of me. Dark enough that I would be able to see any mysterious lights in the sky.

I leaned forward to squint out of my windscreen and satisfied that there was nothing there to see, I sat back again.

The case was closed.

There would be another case tomorrow. In fact, I think Jane said something about an Elf warrior this afternoon.

The End

But do check out the next few pages

There are secrets buried in the Earth's past. Anastasia might be one of them.

The world knows nothing of the supernaturals among them …

… but that's all about to change.

When Anastasia Aaronson stumbles across two hellish creatures, her body reacts by channelling magic to defend itself and unleashes power the Earth has forgotten.

But as she flexes her new-found magical muscle, it draws the attention of a demon who has a very particular use for her. Now she must learn to control the power she can wield as a world of magical beings take an interest.

She may be damaged, but caught in a struggle she knew nothing about, she will rise, and the demons may learn they are not the real monsters.

The demons know she is special, but if they knew the truth, they would run.

Lord Hale's Monster

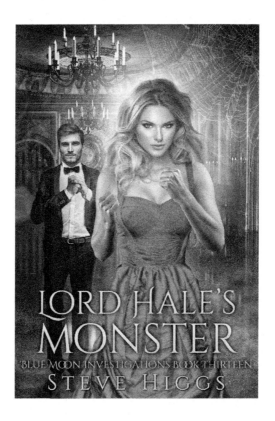

Every second generation of the Hale line dies at the hands of an unnameable monster on his 80th birthday. The current Lord Hale turns 80 this Saturday.

To protect himself, Lord Hale has invited paranormal investigation experts Tempest Michaels and Amanda Harper plus their friends and a whole host of other guests from different fields of supernatural exploration for a birthday dinner at his mansion.

As they sit down for dinner, the lights start to dim and a moaning noise disturbs the polite conversation. Has Lord Hale placed his faith in the right people, or just led them to share his doom?

Finding themselves trapped, Tempest and Amanda, with friends Big Ben and Patience must join forces with a wizard, some scientists, and occult experts, ghost chasers, witches, and other assorted idiots as they fight to make it through the night in one piece.

Could this be their final adventure? Will Tempest finally be proven wrong about the paranormal?

Early Shift

Don't Challenge the Werewolf

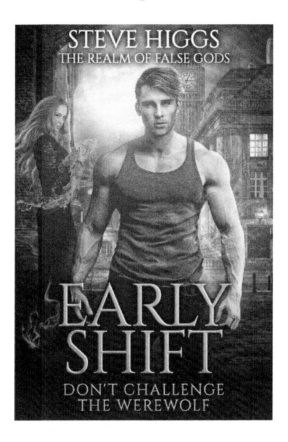

Don't pick a fight with him. You won't lose. You'll die

Zachary has a secret he tries to keep under wraps …

… if only people would let him.

When he drifts into a remote farming community looking for work, the trouble starts before he orders breakfast. Normally he would just avoid the trouble and move on, but there's a girl. Not a woman. A little girl, and the men that want to dominate the village threaten her livelihood.

And that just won't do.

There's something very rotten in this community but digging into it brings him face to face with something more powerful even than him. Something ancient and unstoppable.

He has no choice other than to fight, but who will walk away?

As the false gods find their way into the realm of mortals, how many mortals will rise to defend the Earth?

Be ready for war.

Blue Moon Investigations

Albert Smith's Culinary Chronicles

Patricia Fisher Cruise Mysteries

The Missing Sapphire of Zangrabar

The Kidnapped Bride

The Director's Cut

The Couple in Cabin 2124

Doctor Death

Murder on the Dancefloor

Mission for the Maharaja

A Sleuth and her Dachshund in Athens

The Maltese Parrot

No Place Like Home

Patricia Fisher Mystery Adventures

What Sam Knew

Solstice Goat

Recipe for Murder

A Banshee and a Bookshop

The Realm of False Gods

Untethered magic

Unleashed Magic

Early Shift

Damaged but Powerful

Demon Bound

Familiar Territory

Albert Smith's Culinary Capers

Pork Pie Pandemonium

Bakewell Tart Bludgeoning

Stilton Slaughter

Get sneak peaks, exclusive giveaways, behind the scenes content, and more. Plus, you'll be notified of Fan Pricing events when they occur and get exclusive offers from other authors because all UF writers are automatically friends.

Not only that, but you'll receive an exclusive FREE story staring Otto and Zachary and two free stories from the author's Blue Moon Investigations series.

Yes, please! Sign me up for lots of FREE stuff and bargains!

Want to follow me and keep up with what I am doing?

Facebook

Patreon

Printed in Great Britain
by Amazon

41426221R00138